I0641467

overriding the
extinction scenario

part one

DETECTING
THE BAR ON THE
EVOLUTION OF THE HUMAN SPECIES

KEYS TO
CONSCIOUSNESS AND SURVIVAL
SERIES, Volume 5

Dr. Angela Brownemiller

Metaterra® Publications

overriding the
extinction scenario

part one

DETECTING
THE BAR ON THE
EVOLUTION OF THE HUMAN SPECIES

KEYS TO
CONSCIOUSNESS AND SURVIVAL
SERIES, Volume 5

Dr. Angela Brownemiller

Metaterra® Publications

Metaterra® Publications
OVERRIDING THE EXTINCTION SCENARIO, Part One
Detecting the Bar on the Evolution of the Human Species

KEYS TO CONSCIOUSNESS AND SURVIVAL SERIES: Volume 5
Copyright © 2021, 2020. 2015, 2016, 2017, 2018, 2019, Angela Browne-Miller. Angela Brownemiller
Copyright © 2021, 2020. 2000, 2005, 2010, 2015, 2016, 2017, 2018, 2019, Metaterra® Publications.
All rights reserved in all formats and in
all languages and dialects known or not known at this time.
Published in the United States by Metaterra® Publications.

Dr. Angela BrowneMiller
OVERRIDING THE EXTINCTION SCENARIO, Part One
Metaterra / Angela Brownemiller /Angela Browne-Miller —
1. Survival. 2. Evolution. 3. Consciousness. 4. Psychology. 5. Biology.
6. Ecology. 7. Future. 8. Spirituality. 9. Metaphysical. 10. Interdimensional.
11. Science. 12. Science Fiction.
Library of Congress Control Number: (see website listed above)
ISBN-13: 978-1-937951-16-0 (Paperback on Amazon)
See Amazon for Ebook.
Published in the United States of America for US and worldwide distribution.
Metaterra® Publications.
Cover and content, text and illustrations/graphics,
by and copyright ©Angela Brownemiller.
Book and cover design by and copyright ©Angela Brownemiller.
Ordering information and bulk ordering information available through:
Amazon Paperback and Amazon Kindle.
Also contact
HYPERLINK "Info@Metaterra.com" Info@Metaterra.com

Figure 1:
Welcome To The Portal

"I am optimistic that we will one day have a science of consciousness, but it won't be science as we know it today. Nothing less than a revolution is called for, and it's already on its way."

Dr. Philip Goth
Consciousness and Fundamental Reality

"Evolution is said to have generated millions of biological species here on Earth, millions of life forms occupying, even generating, millions of Earthly niches. Of these millions of species, some 99 percent of these are now extinct. ... Parallel to our own species' biological evolution here on Earth, we can perhaps evolve (or rediscover) for ourselves a continuum of non-physical options here and beyond this physical plane, where we may find we actually already do live and can survive. This may be one of the most pressing truths about ourselves living in this intense time we call 'now.' We walk in at least two worlds...."

Dr. Angela Brownemiller
Keys to Consciousness and Survival Series

EYE OF LIFE

in the
   eye of life
      living
         visions

      rivers of time
        carry
        truth
        rising

        elevating
            light
            life
            survival

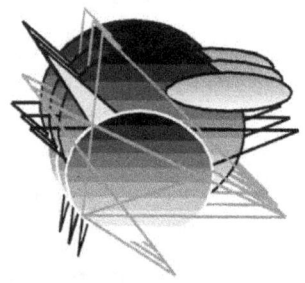

Figure 2:

Keys Of Mind

Table Of Contents

Table Of Illustrations And Diagrams

Illustrations By The Author, Angela Brownemiller©
Unless otherwise noted below* (Figures 7, 12, 17)

Figure 3:
Being Beyond Soma

INTRODUCTION TO
OVERRIDING THE EXTINCTION SCENARIO, Part One

DETECTING
The Bar On The Evolution Of The Human Species

This is a cry from life on Earth to itself, and to anyone out there who may be listening. HELP. Species are dying out, one by one, right before our eyes. What species is next? Are we Humans in line?

Do we need help? Are we in trouble here? Can we truly see all that is affecting us? Do we really know what all is taking place? Do we have the mind/brain capability and capacity to truly know? Are we Humans able to know what we need to know to survive? Is our environment changing in ways that threaten us: Is this a development far more profound than we can detect, far more than we can "see" that it is? Will we and our biosphere survive climate and other environmental, geopolitical, even cosmic, changes? Can Human ingenuity immediately and without hesitation rise to meet the challenges we face?

Yes, yes, yes, and yes to all the above and more.

There is nothing stopping we Humans here on Earth from working together to design and implement major steps to protect ourselves, to save ourselves, is there? Is there? Or are we stopping (or slowing) ourselves?

15

Or is something else, perhaps deep within us, within our own programming, stopping (or slowing) us from saving ourselves from our own extinction?

We do have time, we can still make profound changes and make a difference. Starting immediately, not later, but now, we can join with every nation in the world to do everything it takes to save this biosphere, its livability for ourselves and others.

We can immediately make drastic efforts to begin drawing large amounts of CO_2 out of the atmosphere: we can reforest the planet right away; we can plant millions, even billions of trees a year, every year. This alone can alter profoundly the trajectory of our atmospheric changes. Humans can reforest the planet, rapidly reforesting in places all over the world to, even within one year, plant an area equal to the size of the U.S. and larger. As this reforestation plan only works if the world's existing forests are at the same time being preserved from this moment on, absolute protection of existing forests everywhere, of course including around the Amazon and in all tropical forest areas, must take place immediately.

Agriculture can rapidly adapt to atmospheric changes, for example by fully utilizing the "carbon dioxide fertilization" function that takes place as there are higher levels of carbon dioxide in the atmosphere, levels that cause the photosynthesis of plants to be more efficient and plants to

require less water while being more productive at higher atmospheric temperatures.

We can establish water desalinization plants all over the world, securing fresh water for trees and sustainable agriculture programs, as well as for ourselves. We can place chips and bits of protective screening over our poles to slow and even begin to reverse the melting of the ice caps. We can even form new glaciers with advanced cooling technologies.

We can make a number one funding priority gasoline powered vehicle buy backs, with support for acquiring electric and especially solar vehicles.

We can be concurrently massively, extensively, adding onto public transportation, and providing financial aid to individuals and to nations who require assistance to be rapidly moving in these directions, with globally enforced penalties placed upon those individuals, nations, and corporations who do not comply with these efforts by global deadlines.

And this is just a piece of the picture of immediate steps nations of the world can work together to implement.

However, the Human Species is not moving this quickly, and rather is fighting among its subgroups regarding all levels of these and related steps, including regarding these steps' validity and necessity.

IT IS TIME WE SEE

No matter how we Humans proceed with steps to address maintaining a livable and even breathable environment, it is time we see more about who and what we are.

We are individual living beings, and we are also part of larger lifeforms, such as the Human Species, and the living biosphere. In a sense, we are somewhat like a cell of a jelly fish, a cell in a cell-linked colony whose ultimate survival may be related to all others' survival. As a cell, we have so much information about this interdependence recorded in our genetic record, our biological programming.

Here, I want to note that, using the cell as a model, we also happen to carry the genetically programmed-in cell death function. This function serves in various ways in unicellular and multicellular organisms. Trees shed their leaves, tadpoles lose their tails as they become frogs.

Programmed-in cell death disposes of cells that are no longer needed, or that are dangers to the organism. Basically, cell suicide, apoptosis,[1] is viewed as a necessary function. Many cells in our bodies are *programmed to undergo apoptosis when they should no longer be part of the organism, our body.* Such

---

[1] Cell suicide or its best understood form, apoptosis, is not necrosis. Necrosis takes place when external effects, such as injury or toxins, damage and then kill a cell. Unlike necrosis, cell suicide is internally designed and implemented.

genetic programming has likely been "evolved" into us and other lifeforms.

However we have acquired the programming to be capable of apoptosis, we are programmed to carry this cell level cellular suicide function.

WHY THE DIE OUT?

So now, let's shift the focus of our lens back up to the species level, and even to the biosphere level. Our species, even our biosphere, are living organisms. Human beings are, in many ways, like some of their cells.

Now, let's ask, do we, as species level cells, obediently carry the cell suicide function, carry this function as a species? If so, we must wonder: Are we programmed to die out? Indeed, this is one of my primary questions here in this book.

This is quite a question: Do we carry a deep programming, one we somehow evolved or otherwise acquired, to die out? If so, how and why did we acquire this cell/species suicide programming? Did we develop this during evolution? Would we have chosen to include a die out function within ourselves?

Was there any choice involved? Did the process of "natural" selection naturally select us to be programmed to die out? If the survival of the fittest theory were accurate, wouldn't species have competed to avoid acquiring or evolving programming to die out?

Would they simply have chosen to kill each other when out of room or resources? Would over population and mass die off have been the only alternative?

Have we been programmed to fit this scenario, this range of limited options?

Is it possible we have been programmed, either naturally, or via some form of outside interference, to carry this cell and species suicide function?

What can we do once we see our programming itself may be leading us down a dangerous path toward extinction if/when the room/resources run low and/or our physical environment becomes unlivable for us?

Can we detect, then change, our cell/species suicide programming to override our extinction? Might we need to be able to do this on an *inter*-dimensional, consciousness-based basis?[2]

Can we understand who and what we truly are in order to survive environmental and other challenges we may someday face—and can we do this before our *not seeing this* risks killing us?

---

[2] I develop this "interdimensional consciousness-based" basis in *Volume 3* in this *KEYS TO CONSCIOUSNESS AND SURVIVAL SERIES,* titled, *UNVEILING THE HIDDEN INSTINCT: UNDERSTANDING OUR INTERDIMENSIONAL SURVIVAL AWARENESS.*

Can we detect what deeply embedded messages are at work upon us? Can we override our own programming if this is hindering our survival options, or even our survival itself?[3]

---

[3] These questions suggest the underlying theme of this book, *OVERRIDING THE EXTINCTION SCENARIO, Part One:* **Detecting** *the Bar on the Evolution of the Human Species,* and its essential sequel, *OVERRIDING THE EXTINCTION SCENARIO, Part Two:* **Raising** *the Bar on the Evolution of the Human Species.*

KEYS TO
CONSCIOUSNESS AND SURVIVAL SERIES

SERIES FOREWORD

Just as the fish itself did not discover water, we ourselves have perhaps inadvertently demonstrated the obvious, which is that we cannot entirely, absolutely, know what all it is "we" are immersed in, nor even what all it is that "we" are.

Ultimately, the question of the hour, the question of our times, the question of our reality, is regarding this thing we call our consciousness. Do we identify with our consciousness, is it *of* us, is it *us*, is it *more* than we are, or is it simply a *side effect* of life?

The question as to whether the amorphous consciousness is itself *derivative* of biology, or is itself *independent* of biology (and perhaps even independent of *what any intelligence can entirely discover of itself from within itself and its tools*), will reveal itself to be irrelevant.

This stunning shift in understanding will happen once we recognize that our elusive consciousness can at any point be redefined, *or redefine itself to itself*—or even shift into (or back into) conceptual and even actual *independence of biology*. We can step out of the dictates of biological, evolutionary, synaptic, and related conceptual controls.

We can shift into existence, concurrent existence parallel to, or even if need be independent of, Human science, religion, philosophy, biology, even of the Human brain itself. We can expand beyond old models of ourselves, leave these behind, much like grown children leaving home.

As they depart, we can and want to speculate that our consciousness-es are in a sense like our children, in that they apparently stem from us—a speculation we assume no machine intelligence (as yet incapable of actual procreation and actual biological parental ties) will ever do unless consciously programmed to be able to do by our children once they consciously leave home, their consciousness-es in tow, growing up to consciously be who they already are.

Get ready, even the Human Consciousness is going to break free of the confines of its hosts here on Earth, biological Humans. It's been a nice visit, but the time may come to go, or at least to expand along the continuum where we actually already do live....

Dr. Angela Brownemiller

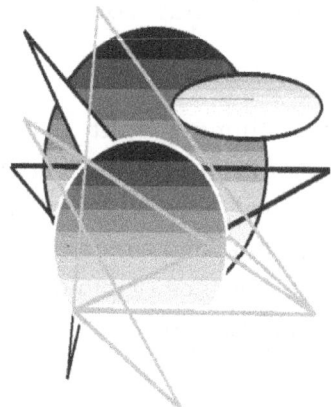

Figure 4:
Keys Of Mind II

αΩα

SECTION ONE

Unveiling
The
Truth
About Our Programming
And Our
Actual Survival Potential

αΩα
Just Imagine

Advancing our own evolution for survival purposes necessitates our further and far more deeply identifying, knowing, tapping into, empowering, and heightening the vast and barely realized capabilities of our magnificent Human Consciousness.

Imagine if even a small portion of the massive funds governments and corporations spend on space travel were invested in advancing travel by the consciousness itself to the realms of the consciousness itself, and to the "inner" and "outer" realms consciousness itself can identify and access.

What grand and potentially life-saving, even species-saving, expansion we may have within our reach, within ourselves, and within our right to access. We have barely begun to understand and access the nature, brilliance, and power of Human Consciousness.

Of course, just think of the funding debates around the exploration of consciousness that would take place in congresses around the world.

Just imagine what the arguments would be for and against budgeting **consciousness exploration and development** *as not only an additional form of "space" travel (which would be challenging enough to convince many of), but also as defense spending.*

Yet, the defense and protection of the Human Species may require our protection, exploration, and honing of the keen and vast powers of our individual as well as our species consciousness-es.

Human Consciousness is a largely untapped resource, our own resource to ever further unveil to ourselves.

Human Consciousness is a realm where vast tracts of domain remain still largely unexplored. Human Consciousness is a valuable, even essential, resource we must turn to now to help ourselves be ready to break free of and survive possible and actual extinction scenarios.[4]

$$\alpha\Omega\alpha$$

---

[4] Important note: This book does not advocate the use of psychoactive medications or hallucinogenic drugs for the exploration of the consciousness. While I do not in this book take a side in the debate regarding these, and while I do very much acknowledge the valuable work and research being done regarding these, I do herein form and detail my position that more than enough interference in our awareness and consciousness has been and is taking place, and that we need to take away outside and even internal interference in our accessing the full range and capabilities of our own actual consciousness. This prepares us for accessing our SELVES even when we no longer travel in physical bodies.

NOTE I:
THIS IS NOT EXTINCTION

OK Human Species, we're going to have to think the hell out of this survival thing. But we can do this, we CAN survive. Extinction need not be on our agenda.

Now, by THINK the hell out of this, I mean really think (in what may sound to some people to be an unusual way) by reaching beyond what our biological brains and their biochemistries of thinking so far offer us. I suggest that transferring thinking processes to our actual selves, to our non-physical selves, without being bound to physicality, is something we can learn and in fact already do know.

Yes, of course, this calls for at least the imagined if not actual acceptance of our species existing pre- or post-, or in addition to, our biological life form here on Earth. Where actual acceptance is a hurdle, simply IMAGINE your self to be free to live in a biological body with a biological brain, and also to exist outside of physicality, even to come and go to and from these forms.[5]

Once we can transfer our understanding of ourselves, of who and what our life form actually is, to our consciousness-es, free of being tied entirely to our biological bodies and biological brains, we can

---

[5] See opening chapters of this book for discussion of out of body, near death, astral travel, and related experiences: *UNVEILING THE HIDDEN INSTINCT.*

at least conceptually come and go from physicality as needed. Nothing momentous here, simply a shift in thinking key to our survival, simply a shift in understanding regarding who and what we actually are.

So, thinking the hell out of this situation becomes quite simple when we expand the process of knowing, add to what we believe we know, to reach beyond the restrictive domain of the biological brain....

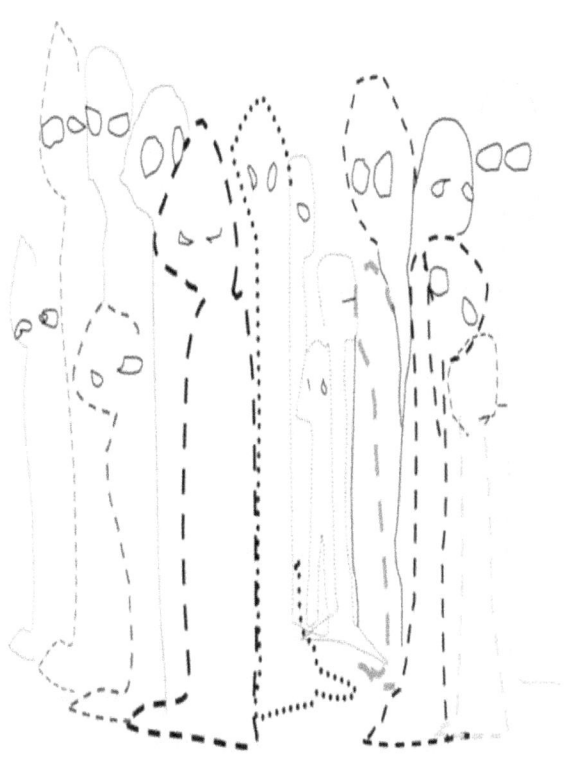

Figure 5:
Species of Consciousness

NOTE II:
This Is Survival

This is in no way an extinction scenario. This is a survival scenario. This is about survival, the survival of the Human Species. It is time we bring these matters to the forefront. This is about our right to understand what our species can do to survive, what the true range of survival options may be.

This is also about our detecting and reaching beyond our biological wiring and brain limitations, programming we may have naturally developed the niche and the genetic code for, or that may have been designed for us, or implanted into us.

This is also about the possibility that we Humans carry or have been implanted with genetic programming that *codes us not to break free of this very programming*. Why? Well, read on and see what this may mean to our species and what we can do about this once we see this. Experience this complex yet simple message unpacking itself through words on these pages, and calling to us from between these lines where the meaning of all this is coming ever more into focus.

Get ready. The following discussion is somewhat a departure from the general thinking of our times, or of any times we have in our recorded Human history here on Earth. (*This thinking may also be regarded by some as a departure from various religious as well as various scientific views, such as those of various evolutionary biologists with their competing theories. However, this book is not intended to take a stand against any viewpoint, rather to ask Readers to think about the possibilities I raise, to just think, even imagine.*)

It is time for the Human Species to consider the concepts discussed

here, to consider what we as a species are indeed able to do, to ask what of our biological wiring and limitations in understanding we can actually rise above.

This book is written for people from all walks of life, and of all belief systems. Readers may be religious or may not be religious, may believe there is a God or that there is not a God. This book does not impose a particular religious, scientific, or other philosophy on its Readers. Rather, Readers are asked to bring what they know and believe to this read, and to hear what this book has to say about the Human Species and the survival of the Human Species.

Indeed, this material is for any and all persons who may want to give some thought to the species survival issues and possibilities discussed herein, whether treating this discussion as scientific, or philosophical, or spiritual, or simply as entertaining fantasy (such as science fiction). Various roads to knowing are welcome.

The Author

Figure 6:
Species of Consciousness II

PREFACE TO
THIS TRUTH ABOUT NOW...

Figure 7: photo courtesy of NASA

Our time here on this Earth is such a momentous journey. For however long our species can be here, riding the wave of this physical existence, we can experience this ride, the commonplace as well as the profound highs and lows of this trip on this remarkable planet.

At some point, maybe even now, we may see signs that perhaps, just perhaps, our species' life in this Earth's biosphere is at risk. We may sense that the quality of our existence here is being compromised, strained. Or we may find that our biosphere is shifting too dramatically for us to physically adapt to these changes in time to survive. Then what? The answer is simple, perhaps too very simple to speak. Extinction is a possibility. We have to admit this to ourselves, to our species.

Of course, for however much time our species has here on this Earth in this physical plane, we can live, even at times love, these grand epochs, millennia, centuries, decades, and even these years on this planet. As we begin to see the pacing of shifts in our environment draw more rapid and or pronounced, we begin to savor the years, yes, and also the seasons, and the months, the weeks, the days, the hours, the minutes, the seconds, the moments as these pass by.

If and when we finally notice this is the **real countdown***, we know, we*

just know. We know that, at some point, we are here in this particular physical, biological, Earthly niche of ours only centuries, then decades, years, months, then minutes and moments before we as the Human Species must either expand to other (conceptual or actual) niches where we can live, or perhaps become entirely extinct.

We do have a choice here. We can choose not to become extinct. *We can choose to rethink, and even to take control of, our own development and/or our own evolution (what ever you, Reader, wish to call it) in order to truly survive. We can choose to see this and then choose to understand what this means. Truly understanding this will be in itself a great step in our own evolution. (For purposes of this book's discussion, I will frequently although not always overlap and merge terms regarding personal and species evolution, adaptation, and development.)*

We can choose not to become extinct.
To avoid extinction,
to survive,
we must adapt in a big way.

Yes, we must consciously adapt in a profound way. This profound and **conscious adaptation** *is indeed possible for us. We can* **choose to adapt***. We can indeed* **choose to choose** *to adapt. We can choose to adapt to immense shifts in our reality so that we can endure and survive in this physical form, or perhaps even in another form should physicality not be an option at that time.*

Extinction is not our only option.

We can consciously and purposefully envision and generate other (physical and non-physical) habitats and niches for ourselves, places where we can go and be safe.

*We must establish safe territories for ourselves, SURVIVAL TERRITORIES[6], **additional (actual and also conceptual) niches** where we can live for a while or for good should we ever need to. (Modern day Earth Human space travel is of course very interesting, however this effort barely touches what this book presents as essential.)*

**We can recognize and establish
as yet not realized safe places, alternate niches,
so that these are ready for us
if and when we ever choose to access these.**

We can and must do this conscious adaptation.

*This is an essential step in Human Species adaptation and ongoing Human Species evolution. We can know that this **access** to safe niches here within as well as beyond this physical plane is our species' birthright. It is time to remember this about ourselves, about our Human Species, about Humanity. We are far more than only a biological life form.*

**We can do this shifting, this conscious expansion.
We are already this mobile.
Our consciousness is already this mobile.**

**We can consciously expand, adapt,
and consciously evolve
to survive.**

---

6 See the *EARTH URGENT TRILOGY* books, also by Dr. Angela Brownemiller, for definition and discussion of these essential SURVIVAL TERRITORIES. Refer to reading list at the end of this present book.

Note III: Awareness of Possibilities

The following book sets forth an **awareness of possibilities** *that we as a species (and as a species among other species also perhaps sensing or considering the matters shared herein) must consider at least in our imaginations, if not also in our hearts and minds....*

****

The following discussion presses gently against the conceptual and actual boundaries of our reality, of our niche, of the niche formed by our consciousness-es. This is not to insult or damage those boundaries, rather to feel how soft, flexible, porous, alive, open to us, within our reach, within the grasp of our vast Human Consciousness, those expansively adaptable boundaries themselves are.

αΩα αΩα
What A Great Experiment

What a great biological experiment our biological evolution here on this Earth has been, and likely still is....

Our evolution, as magnificent as it has been (although highly varying in nature, at least theoretically), has stumbled upon, developed, selected for, or designed, various characteristics of ourselves that are no longer needed (and were perhaps never needed or particularly essential). Examples of these either vestigial- (or simply error-) type organs may include: the appendix, the tailbone, the wisdom tooth. Vestigial organs are frequently described as being: structural remains of lost functions--and or organs remaining in imperfect, flawed, atrophied, or even degenerate forms.

And now, we must ask whether there are other still more useful functions that we may have once had access to, **may have lost or been blocked from continuing full, or even any, actual access to,** *such as: higher more profound intuition, more extensive information processing functions, more* **conscious** *brain "space" to* **consciously** *hold and more deeply examine more incoming information; more rapid brain speed, greater and more* **conscious awareness** *capacity, and so on.*

What higher level functions may have been evolved out of—been broken, damaged, or forgotten, dropped, suppressed, blocked, turned down or off within—our physical (phenotypic) form and its genetic coding? What may have (naturally/accidentally or purposefully) been selected out of us, out of our capabilities, out of our knowing why all this so called "evolution" of us has taken place?

Would our own evolutionary process really have selected to delete or suppress capabilities and awareness-es that may be essential to our species' survival?[7]

And, while so much has been selected out, so much else has been suppressed, buried deeply within us, far beneath the radar of our awareness ... what sort of natural evolutionary process would have implanted into us a quiet controller, a deeply buried executive control function, operating primarily where we cannot see it, far out of our awareness....

We must ask: What is really going on?

---

[7] NOTE: As the term evolution *appears throughout this book, a brief note at the outset of this discussion:*

Evolution is an easy term to toss around, to apply where we wish to apply it. Yet, what this evolution really is, and how this evolution itself came to be, has of course not been absolutely proven, or even agreed to, beyond all doubt. Even classical natural selection theory itself has been debated, adjusted, revised, over time. (Note that Charles Darwin's own theory of evolution was proposed before genes were "discovered.")

Some modern views of evolution include the argument that each evolutionary innovation has made it possible for greater complexity to arise. These views suggest that the emergence or evolution of biological complexity was more than simply the result of random natural selection, and or of random mutation.

However evolution has developed or propelled itself, the actual purpose of evolution itself, how evolution itself arose, remains the question of the hour, at least on the following pages.

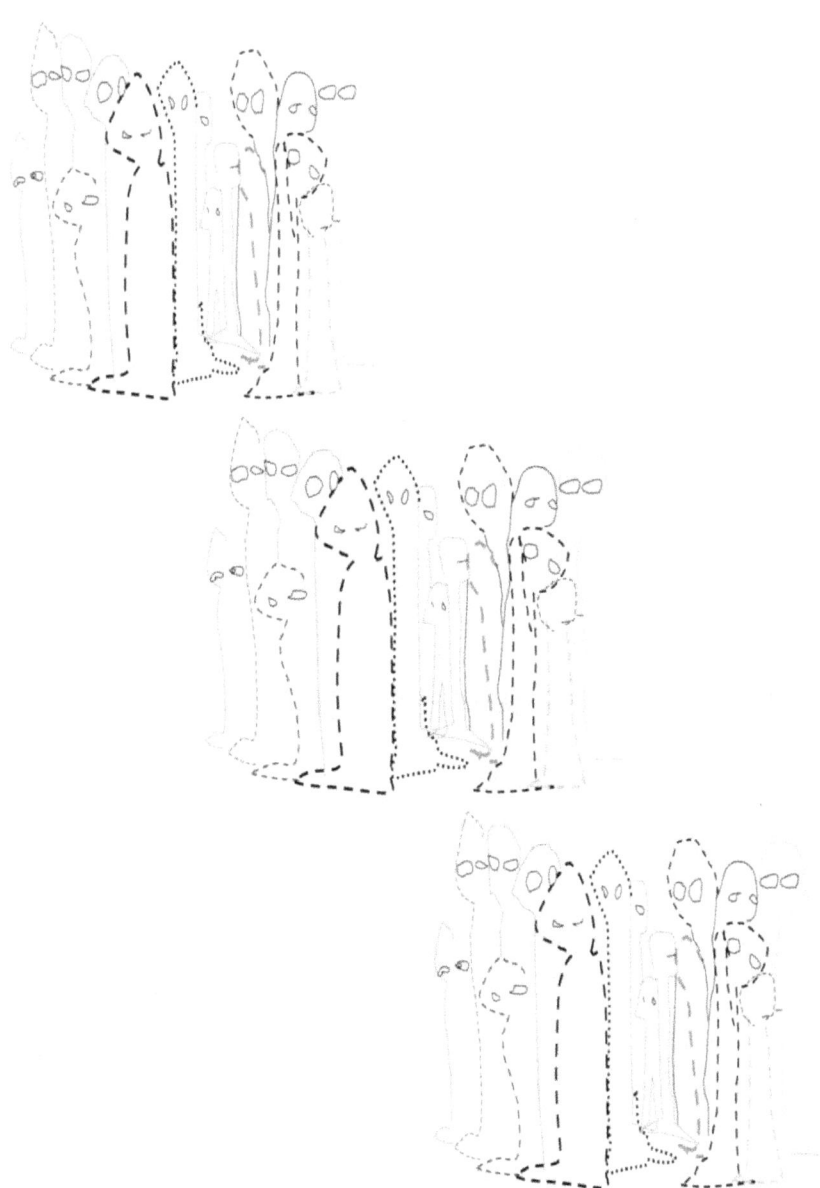

Figure 8:
Species of Consciousness III

R   = revolutionary

E   = evolution

V   = vesting

O   = ourselves in

L   = lateral and

T   = transmigratory

A   = awareness and

S   = survival

αΩα

1
NOTE TO THE "HUMAN" READER

Hello Human Species. We Humans have been here, living in our niche in this physical plane and on this material Earth long enough now to let ourselves remember—and to not allow ourselves to be stopped in taking back—our knowing.

The veils are further lifting. The cave wall is drawing ever more light, and is ever more transparent. Reflections are merging with what they are reflecting, the distinctions between them dissolving yet more clear.

We can begin to see more of what we already know. We can remember who we truly are. We can return in full to ourselves. We are Human Beings, we are Humanity. Our bodies and minds are carriers of this very special life form: the notion, the idea, the spirit, the consciousness—of Humanity itself.

Sure, we have come to think of ourselves as a biological life form. However, our species is beyond biological. I will explain my thinking here on the pages of this book....[8]

---

[8] See further development of these concepts in *Volume 3* of this *KEYS TO CONSCIOUSNESS AND SURVIVAL SERIES*, titled *UNVEILING THE HIDDEN INSTINCT*. Also see reading list at end of this present book.

HUMANITY IS A
LIFE FORM

This life form, Humanity, is not yet entirely understood (or fully remembered) by Human Beings living in biological bodies on Earth. This life form can take physical form and indeed is living on Earth in biologically grown vessels, bodies, yes. Human bodies. This life form is also nonphysical and can move in and out of several planes including this physical plane.

No major realization here, nothing huge to wrap our hearts and minds around. Just think of this nonphysical aspect of who you are, of who we are, as whatever you choose to see this as being. Many Readers are already well on the way, many even already living within this sense of the nonphysical self.

Some call this our awareness or our spirit, or our higher consciousness. Some call this our higher self. Others say the consciousness overlaps with or is the soul. There are many views regarding the non-material side of who we are or may be. I call this truly higher level consciousness we Humans do have, we Humans *actually are*, the True Humanity.

> **Our collective Human Consciousness
> is a life form in itself, a body in itself,
> the true essence of our Human Species.**

WE ARE A
SPECIES OF CONSCIOUSNESS.

This consciousness is who we are far more than our physical bodies are who we are. Our consciousness can live in our physical bodies in order to live here in this physical plane. I say that our consciousness can also *consciously* live beyond this physical plane, as we likely have done many times.

Our consciousness can live in both the physical and the non-physical realms and can do so concurrently, as we already do. And, we can consciously do this, assuming we do choose to realize that we can, **assuming we do choose to take back our knowledge of survival without physical bodies.**

This is actually our true survival, as we are not only our physical bodies. Indeed, we are not really our physical bodies, we are the consciousness-es that inhabit these bodies.

Yes, some Readers will find this a departure from mainstream scientific, religious, and other thinking. Other Readers will not. I welcome you all to join me here. This discussion is to share ideas, to explore possibilities *possibly* relevant to our survival, not to insist upon them.

As I explain in several ways herein, basically, you are your own personal consciousness, which is part of the collective Human Consciousness. You are your own consciousness

living here in your physical Human Body. Feel how you wear your shell, your body, your vessel. Sense how you travel around in physical Human Form with its physical Human Biology including its physical Human Brain. And realize that this physical biological *vessel* itself is not you.

You are the captain of your vessel, not simply your vessel. No matter how much you identify with it (with your physical body's identity), no matter how easy it is to confuse yourself with your physical body, you are not your physical body. If you own a car, you know what this is like, as no matter how much you may identify with your car, you are not your car.

I will say this several times in this and other books, each time to reflect a slightly different aspect of the matters I discuss herein:

Dear Human Reader, as the captain of your vessel, you are your personal consciousness. You are you and you are also more than you. You are an individual and you are also part of a species. You are part of the Human Consciousness Body of the life form of all Humanity. This is your actual species.[9]

THIS MATTER OF CONSCIOUSNESS

The matter of the consciousness has intrigued us for quite some time (intrigued Humans—and yes, perhaps also other

---

[9] This concept is elaborated further in *Volume 3*, titled, *UNVEILING THE HIDDEN INSTINCT*. See the reading list at the end of this present book.

species although other species are not the primary focus of this particular book). Here on Earth, we have sought to understand (via our various religions, philosophies, sciences, even our arts, stories, and imaginations) what this thing we call our consciousness is. We have done this in trying to remember who we are, in trying to access parts of ourselves we may have been blocked from knowing—

blocked because …

**… we (our brains)
have somehow been
randomly
or perhaps even purposefully
evolved and
coded, programmed,
designed,**
not to know.

We are aware that we are aware of ourselves, and we are aware that we think, feel, see ourselves existing. (We have yet to fully understand what *awareness* is, yet we are aware we have awareness.) This awareness is something we are aware of, to some extent. We tell ourselves, "I know him, I know her, I know myself." However, there is far more to be aware of. At any point in time, no matter how much we believe we are aware of, there is always more to know, to sense, to feel.

Awareness can be infinite, and actually is infinite where we choose to know this. There is indeed always more to know about ourselves, more to be aware of.

Note: In the books in this KEYS TO CONSCIOUSNESS AND SURVIVAL SERIES, I have explained my views on consciousness and awareness. In my clinical and research work, I have found **awareness** *itself to be what I call the* **"operant arm of the consciousness."** *In other words, when consciousness is most conscious of itself, it is* **consciousness being aware or having awareness.**

The more aware we are, the more we can participate in what our consciousness "knows and does." I have found that the awareness itself can be trained to become ever more aware of what the consciousness can do, and of who the consciousness, **WE,** *are.*[10]

Moreover, Human Consciousness is much more than we Earth Humans have yet embraced, and than we have yet been allowed to, or have allowed ourselves to, embrace. Human Consciousness is in itself a life form, our life form, *our living presence, our essence.*

This Human Consciousness we as the Human Species carry is quite expansive, is most magnificent, is certainly wondrous. This is Humanity itself. This is also Humanity aware of itself as a life form, as a *body of consciousness* seeking to preserve itself and to survive in this cosmos.

---

[10] I detail more of my thinking regarding consciousness and awareness in several other of my books, such as *UNVEILING THE HIDDEN INSTINCT, Volume 3* in this series, and *SEEING BEYOND OUR LINE OF SIGHT, Volume 10* in this series.

RIGHTFUL PLACE IN
COSMOS

Long has Humanity sought its rightful place in this cosmos. And long has Humanity sought to secure its own niches—the niches it can most likely even generate for itself (by co-evolving along with these niches, and or via consciously generating these niches much like a home builder envisions, then designs, then builds neighborhoods with houses to live in).

Keep in mind that these niches I refer to here, these habitats, are not necessarily only physical plane niches, habitats. The Human Consciousness is not itself necessarily tied only to the physical. The Human Consciousness is an essence that can move from dimension to dimension, to and from physical and non-physical, to and from third and other dimensional realities.

This is not necessarily a complex idea. For example, right now, as you are reading this, you are thinking about this. This thinking itself is taking place and is not entirely physical. Yes, your physical brain is working to compute what you see of these words on these pages into information you can process.

However, the thoughts that form the ideas in your mind, in fact may form even your mind itself, are far more than merely physical. [Several later chapters of this book talk about how our physical brains are designed to "know" (or think they know) a great deal, and yet at the same time, our brains may

actually be designed to stop us from knowing much more. I then, in the next book, *OVERRIDING THE EXTINCTION SCENARIO, Part Two*, explain how our consciousness-es can rise above (designed-in) limitations on our consciousness-es, and thereby raise the bar on our own evolution.[11]]

The idea that Humanity has a rightful place in this interdimensional cosmos is profound and not clear to us as a physical plane Earth based species, which we presently are (or are programmed to believe we are). Why do we not know this as a general part of our living here on Earth? What could be stopping us from fully knowing this? What could be stopping us from fully recognizing the survival implications of fully knowing this?

LONG SOUGHT FREEDOM

The answer is complex, perhaps **even rather revolutionary**. I unpack this matter as this book proceeds. As a starting point to this discussion, let me suggest here that Humanity has likely, often without realizing it is doing so, long sought freedom from its biological limitations, its genetic codings, and even from oppressing and extinguishing forces that we are likely programmed not to recognize.

The very **essence of Humanity**, what Humanity is, and what Humanity has a right to know that it is, is ours because it is who and what we are: Humanity.

---

[11] See reading list at the end of this present book.

Just by existing the way we do, Humanity poses a powerful question to an order where Humanity does not access its full potential. Humanity also poses a powerful question to itself. In fact, I have written this book to talk to Humanity, to help pose this powerful question to Humanity now.

There are territories and bodies, forces and life forms, where and within which the essence of Humanity cannot presently fully travel, even if it needs to. Humanity has, by some mechanism, not been allowed in, has been blocked from full access, and blocked from the full awareness that would provide this access.

Awareness itself is access.

What is holding Humanity back from full awareness of access and therefore from full access? Can the life form, Humanity, come to see what constitutes actual full access?

Is the biological Human Brain designed to restrict access?

I will return to this matter of the biological brain's *restrictions* on us (and how we can override these restrictions) later in this and the following book.

αΩα

2
HUMAN SPECIES ARRIVED HERE ON EARTH TO EVOLVE, NOT TO BE CONFINED

Let's go back to talking about physical Human Beings who are a physical form of the life form, Humanity. Again let me suggest that we are just one stream of the Human Life Form, the stream that arrived in this dimension to, at least in part, develop this aspect of itself here on this physical plane based Earth.

Readers, whether you are reading this book as a philosophical or spiritual inquiry, or as a scientific review, or perhaps as science fiction, let's take some time to, for the sake of this discussion, really consider this possibility....

Again: We Humans are not merely single individual life forms in individual Human bodies. We are part of a larger more interdimensional life form. This life form is that of our physical and also our interdimensional species. We belong to the Human Species here on Earth, and we live here on Earth in the biological Human Bodies that carry us.

Yet, while we did descend to this physical plane to partake in this biological evolutionary process here on Earth, we did not plan or expect to be confined to this niche by forces and

methods—even by genetic and brain programming—developed during the controlled "evolution" we had not anticipated we would face. Perhaps these forces would prefer to suppress us by controlling, even thwarting, our physical evolution on Earth, and by trapping us in a shifting and ever more unstable physical plane biospheric Earth niche.

Whether these suppressing forces are located external to us, or internal (within us, such as in our bio-genetic coding) is almost not the question once we see how "internal" and "external" are simply words. These are simply words invented by biological Earth Humans' 3-D Brains to talk about what those brains think of as differing spaces and their boundaries. Lines between external and internal dissolve in less physical dimensions.

**Now we Humans must resume
control of our own evolution
so that we can remain
captains of our own journeys within,
as well as to and from,
this physical dimension
on this planet Earth and elsewhere.**

It is our right to evolve as well as to travel freely. This book develops this key, even critical, understanding and the value of this understanding so that ...

We can detect and release ourselves from programming that may indeed be designed to confine us (and our awareness-es) to:

> *(a) our particular biological evolutionary path here on Earth; and, to*
>
> *(b) our being just here on Earth rather than coming and going (both physically and non-physically) from this dimension as we choose to, when we choose to, and as we need to in order to survive.*

WE ARE INDEED OUR CONSCIOUSNESS

We Earth Humans are, certainly on some level, aware that we are in essence our consciousness, the species of our Human Consciousness for now living on Earth in our physical biological Human Bodies. On some deep level, deep within ourselves, we do get this truth. Indeed, we have developed religions, philosophies, and techniques such as meditation, attempting to see more of who we are.[12]

---

[12] As I have noted before, yes, these techniques also (according to some) include the use of psychoactive and or hallucinogenic "medicines" or compounds (drugs) as "mind expanding" tools. While I do not herein debate the value of these approaches, I say here, as I have noted in other books in this series, the goal here is to be in **most direct** and highly conscious, highly aware, contact with ourselves, with our minds, with our consciousness-es, unmediated, unmitigated, undrugged, not altered or distorted or obscured by "outside" "influences." Also note that physical plane outside influences such as compounds, medicines, etc. reaching the mind brain through the biological body will not be available to those traveling beyond physical plane existence without biological bodies. Best to learn what this means to the consciousness now, in advance.

Now we can step back and see still more about who we are. We can and must do this greater seeing now.

We are a **colony** of individuated Human Consciousness-es[13] living here on Earth in individual biological Human Bodies with individual biological Human Brains.

Human *Bodies* are housing our species on Earth. I am saying here that: Of course we can live elsewhere and in other ways, and for now we (or many of us) are here living in these Earth Human Bodies.

As members of this Human Colony on planet Earth, we do have individual lives here, yes. And, we are also part of the larger life form we call the Human Species living in this physical plane. We are also part of the still greater and more expansive Interdimensional Humanity Life Form in the interdimensional reality that we call the cosmos.

****

The discussion I offer in this book suggests an expanded definition of who we Humans are, and of Humanity itself. For purposes of the various ideas and discussions I share in this book, the consciousness of this life form we call Humanity —

---

[13] As the individual and the species consciousness are both an individual and a group consciousness, I frequently herein describe our consciousness as consciousness-ES, with the hyphen purposefully included (as in -es). I also frequently follow this form describing our awareness as awareness-ES.

or better stated, this consciousness which *is* Humanity, is what our Human Species is about, is what our Humans Species *is*. Again:

We are a Species of Consciousness. Consciousness is our actual Life Form.

This essence, this presence, I am calling Humanity here is nonphysical in basic nature. However, herein I suggest that our actual species, this very species of the Human Consciousness, Humanity, can physicalize itself as well as take other energetic forms and travel in nonphysical ways. Just see our Human Species living here on Earth as an example of what Humanity can move of itself into, and develop in, the physical plane. Along these lines, I add that we likely can and have similarly developed ourselves outside this physical plane here on Earth, and elsewhere in other physical and nonphysical dimensions.

WE HAVE BEEN RESTRICTED

Now, many people have said at this juncture in my teaching this material that, "Wait, just look around this Earth at all the selfishness, cruelty, and pain. Look at what Human People do to each other and to other animals. If this is what Humanity does here on Earth, what is so great about who we are?"

I say good question. Very good. In fact, this question brings me to further note here the heart and purpose of this book. Herein I explain in great detail my understanding that we

Humans have been **locked into an evolutionary pattern** that has become increasingly mixed, in some ways dangerous for itself, for us, for other life forms joining us here on Earth, even for the Earth's biosphere.

In my years of research and work with the Human Mind, I have come to see that there are indeed possibilities we must at least be aware of. ...

CONSIDER THIS

Consider the distinct possibility that: *Something in our biological brain's wiring, and in the genetic coding for this wiring, is suppressing us ...*

We are coded to hold this suppression within our species, to pass this along through our generations—*whether this coding came to us entirely via genetic evolution, or via some interaction between, even a co-evolving of, our species' genetics and the niche we live in on Earth--**and or in some other still more complex and otherwise driven, or even otherwise motivated, way.***

Again, I want to note this possibility: It may be that either we have evolved this **suppressing limitation** into our coding, or this **limitation may have been implanted** into our coding, or there may be another process at work. (Or perhaps all of the above.)

We must allow for the possibility that not only have there been **mechanisms evolved into, implanted into, our coding**

to place **an** *artificial ceiling on our evolution* (**and an artificial ceiling on our awareness of what is taking place**), this effort has been made to hold us unwittingly captive here in order to confine or even enslave us (our energy, our consciousness-es, our species).

Indeed, once we allow for the possibility, even just the vague possibility, that our genetic coding has been controlled (and or implanted into us) by some form of *intelligent design or perhaps intelligent life form*, **we must remain alert.** (NOTE: Refer to other books in this series where I discuss the overlap between a design and a life form, and explain that a design itself can be its own life form.)

We must at least consider the possibility that, as we become more and more aware of who we are, the *programming implants in our own coding are being amplified* so as to continue to retain control of us, control of Human Beings on Earth and beyond.[14]

CONTROL OF
WHAT IS ALLOWED INTO OUR AWARENESS

As I detail in later parts of this book, this is about *control of what is allowed into our personal consciousness, into our conscious awareness, control of us as individuals and as a species: control of what we know and of what we know we know.*

---

[14] For definition and discussion of this BEYOND, refer to *Volume 10* in this series, titled, *SEEING BEYOND OUR LINE OF SIGHT.* See also *Volume 4* in this series, titled *HOW TO DIE AND SURVIVE.*

Many of us remember the grade school science project where we grew planaria in the biology lab, where we were directed to conduct experiments on this life form in our little circular glass petri dishes.

For those planaria, those petri dishes were the world. There was no escape, no alternative, no other reality. I do not know whether those planaria ever questioned those glass limits, ever wondered if their existences were being "intelligently" controlled and limited. Based on what I was being taught about planaria, I assumed they did not have the capacity to wonder, to ask questions of any sort.

However, one day I did ask my science teacher whether we Humans live in another form of petri dish, whether we might be someone else's experiment. All the kids in class laughed and the teacher thought I was making yet another joke. I was sent out of the room for discipline.

Then, after school, I was made to write 200 times on the chalkboard, "I will not disrupt class." When I added the line, "or think for myself" to this chalkboard writing, I was then further disciplined.

INTERVENING FACTORS

Also consider this *possibility*: There have been serious effects, controls, blocks, interventions, even implantations into our biological Human Forms and Brains. There have been powerful yet subtle, even disguised, intervening forces who have interfered in what could have been the pure, direct,

beneficent, and unimpeded movement of true Humanity into this physical form, into this physical body and brain, and into this physical evolution here on Earth.

My years of social and psychological work with thousands of people dealing with stress, habits, compulsive patterns, addictive problem behaviors, creative and learning blocks, issues of consciousness, and more, and my research into various brain functions (such as memory, cognition, decision-making, creativity, intuition, learning, and behavior) and brain programming (such as habituation, addiction, brainwashing, and other "functions") have led me to see what I now share in later chapters of this and following book: **the distinct and highly programmable nature of our biological brain and the why of this.**

There have been what I find to be significant **evolutionary impediments** to our bringing in full to this physical plane the true essence, quality, and capability of Humanity. There have been factors affecting Humanity's living up to its full potential while in physical form as the Human Species on Earth. As I suggest in the Introduction to this book, there may also be evolutionary, and or other programmed-in, factors bringing the Human Species closer to its own extinction.

Note: Nothing about what I say on these pages relieves Humans of their responsibilities, including to make every effort to protect this Earthly biosphere from Human damage or other problematic Human effects. As I indicate in the Introduction to this book, there are range of immediate and ongoing actions Humans can and in my opinion must take.

αΩα

<u>3</u>
POWERFUL FACTORS ARE DESIGNING AND CONFINING US

Reader, again I note …

Whether as reality or as science fiction, however you choose to serve this to yourself, we must at least allow ourselves to consider the possibilities raised in this book:

We Humans Beings here on Earth may be part of a great experiment. We could be some higher intelligence's petri-dish planaria, or perhaps caged lab rats. We could be a test species, perhaps a species being studied and experimented on to observe its **survival potential.**

THERE MAY BE POWERFUL FACTORS

As "out of this world" as this may sound, we have to at least consider this possibility. This may be relevant to *our surviving extinction pressures*: there may be powerful factors, intelligent factors, intelligences, confining Humanity to its physical Earth form, restricting Humans to only this 3-D niche here on Earth – and or to the physical plane where ever Humanity goes.

Again, this is not to say that we Humans living on physical plane 3-D (third dimensional) Earth should avoid addressing survival here on this 3-D Earth. Not at all. This is, however, to also say that we Humans do best to address survival pressures and options here in the 3-D physical plane *as well as in dimensions beyond 3-D, realms where our consciousness-es can also take us once trained to do so, realms where we actually already do live.*

TAKING ALL THIS IN

That there may be factors restricting our survival potential is an unusual idea. How do we take this in? What does this mean to us? What can we do about something this unclear to us?

The first thing we can do is to begin to explore this understanding. Being so <u>programmed not to know</u> something means that we have to take this opening in our awareness in steps, allow ourselves to consider all this as easily and gently as we can.

I suggest we just think about the possibility that these factors implement their restricting of us by preventing us, we Humans, from freely and fully (if at all) accessing KEY parts of our consciousness-es and "natural" awareness-es, our actual "intelligences" that allow us to know, to remember the full range of Humanity, and to remember forms and options and niches that we Humans can indeed live in and even create for ourselves.

TO OVERRIDE

To OVERRIDE the direction and progression of the evolutionary and historical train or ship we are riding, we must become aware we are passengers heading to a location we may not have selected for ourselves, perhaps a degraded biosphere or perhaps extinction itself.

We need not be
caged hamsters trapped
on a tread mill
nor
ants programmed to
march in a death spiral
with no exit.

If we are actually lab rats, <u>beings trapped in an experiment</u> of some sort, can we discover this about ourselves, about the survival pressures we are facing or soon to face? Can we break free before it is too late? Can we see what is happening, see very soon now so we can survive extinction pressures?

COULD IT BE

Could it be that we are trapped in a *species extinction experiment* so massive we cannot see it houses us, encompasses us, even directs us, and continues to do so as long as we do not see it?

Could it be that the *key to rising above this experiment*, breaking free of what experimenters have programmed for us, programmed into us, is our taking fully heightened, fully *conscious* **control of our own awareness, our own consciousness, our own evolution—our own ability to consciously and rapidly adapt as needed**?

We must recognize within our programming, within our coding, within this evolution-extinction laboratory we call our Earth biosphere, any implanted, obscure but (past or present) impeding interventions for what these are.

We must see these interventions into our species' development and evolution in order to overcome the limitations these interventions have imposed upon us, and that we have obediently imposed upon ourselves, our species.

We CAN overcome **implanted evolutionary designs** by recognizing these, by being aware of what these can be and do within and to us. Once we recognize these implanted designs, we can rise above the invisible programming hiding itself within us, **camouflaging itself as ourselves**. We must now see that:

**WE ARE NOT
OUR PROGRAMMING.**

**WE ARE NOT OUR PATTERNS.
WE ARE NOT OUR BEHAVIORS.**

WE ARE NOT WHO
WE HAVE BEEN PROGRAMMED
TO THINK WE ARE.[15]

We must see what is going on to free ourselves here and elsewhere. We must see this to take back Humanity's rightful place in this physical dimension on Earth and elsewhere, yes, in this interdimensional cosmos.

**We must see this to
captain our own
evolution now,
to activate
our ability
to purposefully adapt.**

---

[15] The matter of our being programmed to confuse ourselves with our emotional and behavioral patterns, habits, and addictions is explained in *Volume 10* of this series, *SEEING BEYOND OUR LINE OF SIGHT*, and *Volume 3* of this series, *UNVEILING THE HIDDEN INSTINCT*, and also in *Volume 8* of this series, *NAVIGATING LIFE'S STUFF, Book One*. Refer to reading list at the end of this present book. See also books in the companion series, *FACES OF ADDICTION*, specifically the volume titled, *SEEING THE HIDDEN FACE OF ADDICTION: DETECTING AND CONFRONTING THIS INVASIVE PRESENCE. See DrAngela.com for more information.*

Even if our evolution is itself
the experiment
we are the subjects of,
once we see this,
once we are aware of this,
we can find a way
out of this laboratory process.

We can
override any
troubled evolutionary path,
any extinction scenario,
we may be facing
or generating
or somehow
buying into.

WE HUMANS CAN
FREE OURSELVES

We Humans can call forth our finest essence and true interdimensional nature, our true Humanity itself. This is who we are—and who we may need to know we are to survive.

We can call ourselves forth. We can and must do this to develop ourselves in a direction that can free us of the limitations we have been coded, programmed, to evolve into ourselves.

And, we can and must do this to free ourselves of any limitations that have been planted within our biological brains and our genetic codings, and into our biological development (and evolution) processes here in this Earthly region of the physical plane.

We are this powerful Species of Human Consciousness, of Humanity. This Humanity must be freed to be itself, and to truly survive changes in its physical, emotional, mental, energetic environments. We are all on this survival drive together, all Humanity is facing the same possible extinction scenario.

Humanity is the finest and core essence of this magnificent Human Species we are part of. And Humanity is calling us to ourselves, and to our rightful place in this **interdimensional ecosystem** of which we are part.

WE ARE CALLING
OURSELVES

This is in essence a call to arms. However, the arms I speak of here are not what traditional freedom fighters here on physical plane Earth may carry. The arms I refer to are not the guns, missiles, and bombs we have seen in Earth warfare. The

arms I refer to here are the essential *power tools of profoundly heightened awareness* and focused energies that come with this awareness.

Being fully conscious
and fully able to apply this consciousness
to survive
is being armed.
Being armed is greatly heightening our awareness
to truly see what is actually going on.

And, if we do discover we are subjects in massive
SPECIES EXTINCTION TRIALS,
we can arm ourselves with the
full power of our true
Human Consciousness
TO SURVIVE, AND TO
RAISE THE BAR ON THE
EVOLUTION OF THE HUMAN SPECIES.

IT IS TIME NOW TO DETECT AND
OVERRIDE THE EXTINCTION SCENARIO.

αΩα

SECTION TWO

We Can And Must
Take Control
Of Our Own
Evolution
As A
Species Of Consciousness

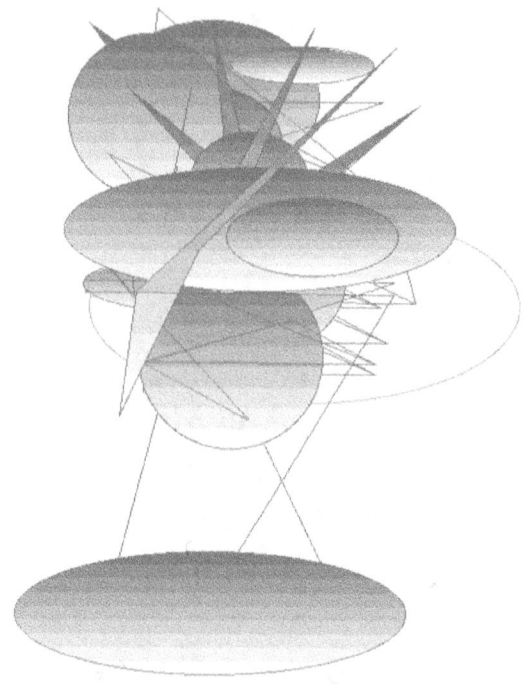

Figure 9:
Mind Of Evolution

αΩα

4
OUR EVOLUTION IS OURS
(OR CAN BE)

This is about you. This is about all of us. We need you, we need us—all of us—*to assume control of our own evolution as a species of consciousness.* We *can* do this. And we must do this to fortify and preserve the Human Species, to allow our species to truly address possibly critical survival pressures.

This is about our developing new approaches to our survival here on Earth, and new approaches to our survival in other (multi- and inter-dimensional) niches, locations of our consciousness, we may need:

(a) to recognize, and travel back and forth from;

(b) perhaps even first to actually conceive of, to generate and then find;

(c) perhaps even to further develop these location options in case we do find the need to expand into or even relocate ourselves, our awareness-es, "out there."[16]

---

[16] See the definition of the **continuum of consciousness** in *Volume 10* in the *KEYS TO CONSCIOUSNESS AND SURVIVAL SERIES*, titled, *SEEING BEYOND OUR LINE OF SIGHT*.

I offer the discussion in this book to allow us to think ever more carefully, and in new ways, about the tremendous and as yet largely unexplored yet essential capacity of our Human Consciousness to meet survival challenges we may face.

BEYOND THE BOUNDARIES OF OUR BIOLOGY LIES THE UNTAPPED RESOURCE OF
OURSELVES

Advancing our own evolution for our survival purposes necessitates our further and far more deeply accessing, and identifying, recognizing, tapping into, also exploring, empowering, heightening — our Human Consciousness.

Imagine if the massive funds governments and now also corporations spend on space travel were turned to *travel by the consciousness itself to the realm of the consciousness itself* or to what I have elsewhere defined as the *continuum of consciousness.*[17] Imagine the profound budgetary dilemma regarding the funding of exploration of something we cannot locate on, or direct ourselves to, via 3-D maps.

We Humans must expand our understanding of our nature to see that: (a) we are far more than physical beings inextricably tied to biology; and, (b) we are not only far more than biological, we are a *species of consciousness* itself.

---

[17] See again *Volume 10* in this series, *SEEING BEYOND OUR LINE OF SIGHT.*

I say we can come face to face with our consciousness, we can come into greater contact with ourselves, access our consciousness far more fully and directly than we are thus far genetically and neurally wired to do, far more than our biological brains presently allow us to do.[18]

We can overcome barriers to our accessing the full potential of our Human Consciousness, the potential we have a right to as it is ours. These are barriers that have developed either: (a) by a random accident of nature; (b) by some form of "natural" evolution (or even co-evolution among species and environments); and or, (c) by some "design," some "intelligent" factor or force, performing some direction of--or implant into--us, into our genetic coding, and into our evolution itself.

Once we can directly access *us*, open any locked gates to ourselves, and to full access to our own multi-dimensional consciousness-es, we can do what we need to do to truly survive.

We *can* access and exercise the great capacity we carry deep within ourselves. We can *consciously* apply our *complex*

---

[18] As I suggest in other books in this series, it is the **awareness function** of our consciousness that allows us to know we have a consciousness, to be AWARE we have a consciousness, to be CONSCIOUS so to speak. I call our **awareness** the **operant arm** of our consciousness, and say that we can expand our **operant awareness** to a far greater capability in order to activate the knowledge deeply carried within our consciousness. See *Volume 3* in this series, titled, *UNVEILING THE HIDDEN INSTINCT.*

consciousness to address what we may need to address, including to recognize, understand the real nature of, survive, and override, any form of *extinction process or program,* any *extinction scenario* we may at some time face (or may be presently facing).

Human Consciousness is a largely untapped resource, a realm where vast and magnificent <u>tracts of domain</u> remain still largely unexplored, a resource we must access and turn to now to help ourselves be ready to survive possible and actual extinction scenarios.

Note: These tracts of domain are present along and within our CONTINUUM OF CONSCIOUSNESS. (See definition and description of this continuum in Volume 10 in this series, SEEING BEYOND OUR LINE OF SIGHT.)

MANY VIEWS RESTRICT OUR CONSCIOUSNESS TO OUR BIOLOGY

Much of the present time "modern" discussion of Human Consciousness refers to the biology of this consciousness and tells us that our consciousness is not only biologically based, but is entirely *biologically generated*. (See Figure 14 later in this book for description of options beyond simple biologically based consciousness.) This view generally says that our consciousness is produced by our biological brain.

(As I detail in later chapters of this and the following book, my view is that our biological brain itself may actually be designed, or may have actually designed or evolved itself for various reasons, to *limit our direct and fully conscious access* to our actual non-biological selves, which is what and who we actually are.)[19]

Of course, the view that our consciousness stems *entirely from and is based entirely within our biology* is a powerful perspective. This view dominates our understanding of who we are and of what we can do.

**Our biological brain is programmed to tell us
we are biological.
This makes sense, from the brain's perspective.
And of course, as biological life forms
living in biological bodies,
this is what our brain knows us to be:
biological life forms.**

This view holds that our brain, and the mind, even the consciousness that we have, arises from this biological brain. Extensions of this view add that, as the frontal lobe, forebrain area, of our brain has evolved, so has our consciousness.

---

[19] Again, refer to *Volume 3* in this series, *UNVEILING THE HIDDEN INSTINCT: UNDERSTANDING OUR INTERDIMENSIONAL SURVIVAL AWARENESS*, for further discussion and explanation of our "non-biological" selves.

So, from this biological origin of Human Consciousness standpoint, as our biological brain evolves then so does our consciousness arise and follow. This standpoint says that: without our biology we do not have a consciousness; and that, if we are not biological, we perhaps do not exist.

My extension of this view, discussed later in this and the following book, says that if indeed there is, was, or can be a biological basis of our Human Consciousness, then we ourselves do have an option. We can choose to assume we are restricted to only our physical plane basis, that this is our past, present, and future reality and that is that.

Or, we can choose to expand ourselves to be both physical and non-physical beings who can be tied to our biology as needed, and also not tied to our biology should we wish to or need to be independent of biology and still exist. We can consciously walk in two worlds, see where we already do live. We can know this about who we are every day we live here and beyond.

We can purposefully further adapt and evolve access to our consciousness both via our biological brain, and beyond our biological brain. (See again figures and chapters later in this and the following book.)

In other words, let's say our consciousness is there, here, is who we actually are. If so, we can consciously choose whether we wish to restrict our own access to ourselves to only our biological brain. We can also explore, allow ourselves to

know or develop, additional options for ourselves, expanded definitions of ourselves as life forms not entirely bound or defined by biology.

We can live concurrently here, and beyond, as we already do. Now we can consciously assume our place along our continuum of consciousness, knowingly occupying our place.

OTHERS
RESTRICT
OUR CONSCIOUSNESS TO
RELIGION OR SPIRITUAL PHILOSOPHY

There are of course those who do suggest that the consciousness (or spirit or soul by some definitions) is: beyond "here," in heaven for example; and/or existed and still exists prior to and independently of us as biological Human Beings.

This sort of view involves the conceptual (and actual) separation of the origins of our consciousness from our biological development and evolution. From this standpoint, the sky or the cosmos is the limit as the consciousness is free of its biological (and perhaps of any) evolution.

However, for the most part, this same consciousness is *apparently tied to a God or to some form of spiritually-defined being.* (Some even call this a "God-based consciousness.") Of course, if one does truly equate "higher" consciousness with a god or other divine being, this very popular view (or as some would call it, "original" view) may at least partially

turn the tables away from the confining view that consciousness requires biology, that consciousness must be, and only be, biological.

Yet, most divine being, God-based, views tend to require of followers that they worship specific divine God-like being or beings, and belong to the religion or spiritual philosophy that defines for them their divine being or beings. It is only when belonging to the given particular belief system that there is some upholding of a non-biological aspect of consciousness. Here, belief in a higher divine being is the path to non-biological life.

While this view is a powerful step toward finding our non-biological selves, this view tends to *restrict or control our full and direct access* to our full and fully empowered consciousness. This view says that this access is gained *only* through the doors religions and or spiritual dogmas like religions prescribe. This view is telling us that access to the soul, or to the afterlife itself, is attained via a belief in a God, a divine being, more powerful than oneself.

However, this view is a detour from the self to the self. This view is not direct access by oneself to one's own aware consciousness. This view tends to say we do not have a right to go there, even cannot go fully there, without the given belief in the given God.

While I have no particular problem with most spiritual and religious belief systems, I do have a serious concern that we are too

frequently told that we require an intermediary to contact our own consciousness, that we cannot get there entirely directly, independently. (The notion that we require a gatekeeper to what we carry within us, to our SELF, even to our consciousness, can be questioned. Similarly, the notion that our brain's executive serves as gatekeeper to our own access to our SELF, even to our consciousness, can be questioned.)

ALL HUMANS HAVE A RIGHT TO ACCESS THEIR CONSCIOUSNESS

Another concern to consider here is this: a religion- or dogma-as-access standpoint is a model that can be quite exclusionary. This model says there is only one path, or one type of path (a path of belief and adherence to prescribed beliefs, attitudes, and behaviors) to access one's own consciousness, one's own non-physical self, even one's own possibility of an afterlife.[20]

While I welcome Readers of all belief and non-belief systems to this book, I do want to share my response to any exclusionary dogma-dictated path to consciousness: I say that a dogma- or religion-dictated approach may leave people out, and is not only unfair but not accurate.

It is ironic that anyone would even think that either science or religion could seek to close some people out of what they already do

---

[20] See discussion of the ***afterlife possibility*** in other books in this *KEYS TO CONSCIOUSNESS AND SURVIVAL SERIES*, such as *Volume 10*, titled, *SEEING BEYOND OUR LINE OF SIGHT.*

carry within themselves, lock them out of their own consciousness.

How can anyone shut anyone else out of what is already right there within that person? *(Later in this and the following book, I do examine in detail how it is actually the biological brain itself that may be shutting us out of full and direct access to our own consciousness.)*

Ideally, all Humans, whether or not religious or spiritual per se, have a right to fully know and fully access their consciousness-es.

This book (as do other books in this *KEYS TO CONSCIOUSNESS AND SURVIVAL SERIES*) suggests that we can choose to view consciousness as arising independent of biology, however, not necessarily or only via god-like forces or other higher intelligences. Discussion from this standpoint grows on the one hand quite dicey and on the other quite freeing. This perspective is perhaps the most user friendly in terms of *readily accepting everyone into the realm of the consciousness, of their own consciousness, where they already do live.*

WE CAN
BREAK FREE

But back to biology a moment. As biological Human animals, we do believe that (are programmed to, wired to, believe that) we take in and process what we know only via our biological senses and our biological brains. So, the first of the views

above, that of the biological origin of consciousness, is perhaps easier for many people to take on, easier for their biological brains to accept or allow.

And, of course, our biological brain does seek to dominate our perceptions. Our biological brain tells us *that* we think, and tells us *what* we think, and even tells us that *we believe* we are basically biological beings. This brain says to us, "I am, therefore you think. I, your biological brain is what thinks. You exist because I exist. Without me, you do not exist."

Whether or not they realize it, many Readers are familiar and rather comfortable with the popular notion that our consciousness is biologically based and derived from our biology and our biological brains.

After all, many ask, how can we exist without our biological bodies? Whether or not this biological explanation explains everything about our consciousness, and whatever (if any) side of this ongoing discussion you, Reader, are presently on, I am saying in this book that:

**We now have the ability to
consciously and purposefully
develop, evolve, ourselves,
our aware consciousness…**

**…to expand beyond the confines of
biological (as well as non-biological)
boundaries and limits on our consciousness.**

**We can consciously locate ourselves along our own
CONTINUUM OF CONSCIOUSNESS
where we already do exist.**[21]

Regarding biological constraints on our evolution, I suggest that: our Human Consciousness is developed enough (and/or evolved enough) to choose to choose to evolve itself, to **assume control of itself**, beyond whatever ties to biology, or restrictions of biology, it may have here on this physical Earth. I add that:

**Our Human Consciousness
can learn to be, or to more fully become,
what it truly is:
an *independent* life form,
one not necessarily
dependent upon the
biological body and brain presently housing it.**

And we must do this now, we must take control of our own consciousness to evolve it past any biological limits it may be experiencing (whether we inadvertently built, evolved, these limits into ourselves, into our brains, or have had these limits imposed upon us or coded into us).

---

[21] See my definition and discussion of this *continuum of consciousness* in other books in this series such as the volume titled, *SEEING BEYOND OUR LINE OF SIGHT.*

On some level we know this, because we *are* this, *we are this independent life form* of Human Consciousness. Let's regain this knowing and be who we truly are here in this physical Earth biosphere as well as everywhere else we may choose to concurrently exist, everywhere we can *conceive of* as existing.

αΩα

5
OUR BRAIN'S OPERATIONAL AWARENESS MUST BE FURTHER EVOLVED

Science seeks to identify specific operational linkages between the biological brain and the mind. Cognitive science seeks to define specific areas and actions in the brain that account for specific cognitive phenomena. What is clear is that the precise brain (biological, neural, biochemical, bioelectrical) functions that result in specific thoughts, cognitions, mental processes, are not (not yet if these ever will be) precisely and entirely defined or definable. Rather, what is best ascertained is the "operational approach" or general correspondence between cognitive and electromagnetic data. Ultimately, the relationship, even the link, between mind and brain is said to be "operational."

Operations of our biological brains may or may not explain all or even most of our minds, let alone of our consciousness-es, whatever these actually are. I continue to contend that we can do as we choose to with our consciousness-es, even evolve these in ways and directions not yet realized or implemented. Here is where I offer the notion of the *operant awareness* as the *operating arm* of the consciousness. Hence, I say in this book series, more fully heightening and activating our *awareness functions* can give us more access to our

consciousness—*and more mobility along our continuum of consciousness.*[22] I also suggest that we are genetically programmed and wired **not to access** our consciousness, not to be fully in command of our own brain/mind operations. The next sections of this and the following book offer scientific information that indicates this.[23]

It Is Time To See
Imagining As Valuable

Here, I want to turn to what I herein describe as the *imagination function,* something that is essential in our lives.

Note that in the previous chapter I write, "…everywhere else we may choose to … exist, everywhere we can *conceive of* existing."

I use the words *conceive of* here to suggest something more about the Human Consciousness. This is a simple notion, as you will see. Think of the **imagination function** our brains and minds have developed and or evolved.

As is the case for many of the traits we have developed or

---

[22] See again, the definition and discussion of this **continuum of consciousness** in other books in this series such as *Volume 10,* which is, *SEEING BEYOND OUR LINE OF SIGHT: CONSCIOUSLY MOVING THROUGH LIFE'S CHANGES, TRANSTIONS, AND DEATHS.*

[23] Refer also to *OVERRIDING THE EXTINCTION SCENARIO, PART TWO,* which is *Volume 6* in this *KEYS TO CONSCIOUSNESS AND SURVIVAL SERIES.*

evolved into ourselves, we likely have this imagination function because it is useful, because it has **survival value**. Perhaps we somehow managed to retain this powerful imagination function deep within our coding, even within our consciousness, for a time when we might need to access its full power. If this function is key to our realizing what is actually happening to us, it could be that the power of this function has been suppressed or denied us by forces or factors interfering with our evolution and wiring.

ABOUT THIS THING
WE CALL REALITY
WHICH APPARENTLY
IS NOT
IMAGINATION

Science tells us that our brain distinguishes between imagination and what we call "reality." Of course, as I have elsewhere explained in depth, the brain suggests to us (tells us) who and what we are as physical biological beings, thereby controlling our sense of reality out the gate.[24]

Our brain's defining of reality differs from the imagin-*ing* of something. Let's start with reality, or what our brain tells us is reality. I of course here simplify a whole scientific explanation for the sake of brevity:

Visual information (perceptions processed into data bits)

---

[24] Refer to the early chapters of *Volume 3*, titled, *UNVIELING THE HIDDEN INSTINCT.*

from what our brain and science tell us are "real" events flows into the brain. The brain is already determining what it is perceiving (defining) as reality, sending this information "up" from the brain's occipital lobe[25] (the visual processing center in the rear area of the brain), "up" to its parietal lobe[26] (located in the "rear top area of the brain" in front of the occipital lobe, between the occipital lobe and the frontal lobe).

Basically, our brain is wired to, programmed to, process our sensations and perceptions to define a physical plane reality, the reality we are told by our brains to accept as reality. Part of this definition of physical reality for us is our brain's definition of us to us as being IN-body life forms, physical biological life forms.[27] (I have detailed my theory regarding our brain's generation of our sense that we are physical beings in other books in this series such as *UNVEILING THE HIDDEN INSTINCT*.)

---

[25] There are four lobes of the brain: the frontal, parietal, temporal, and occipital lobes.

[26] The parietal lobe is located in the top back of the brain and is divided into two regions: one involves sensation and perception to form a single perception or cognition, the other involves integrating sensory input primarily from the visual cortex, forming a sort of spatial coordinate system to represent (define) the world around us. Again note, as I explain in the books in this series, our brain constructs a reality we are told by our brains to accept as reality. IMPORTANT NOTE: Even what I call our IN-body sensations are set up by our brains, programmed by our brains for us to believe is our reality. (See again, *Volume 3*, titled, *UNVEILING THE HIDDEN INSTINCT.*)

[27] I define this process in detail in the opening chapters of *Volume 3*, titled, *UNVEILING THE HIDDEN INSTINCT.*

THE BRAIN'S GESTALT ILLUSION
AS REALITY

When our brain does not have enough data or enough interpretable data to give us a full picture of what our brain is telling us is our reality, our brain fills in the gaps, much like this basic diagram suggests:

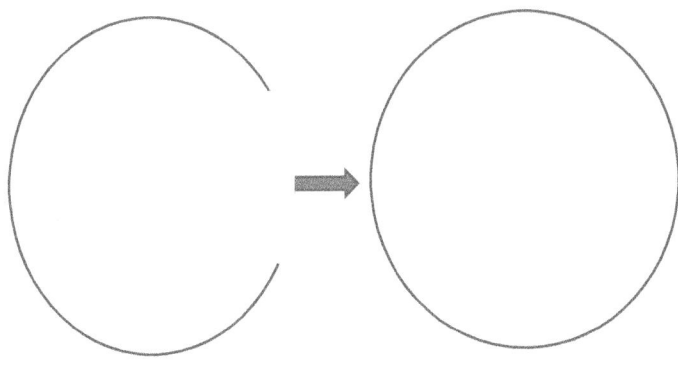

Figure 10:
Form Completion Function

The diagram above shows the closing of a broken circle, which is, in simple terms, the brain's completing a picture of reality when it does not have full enough information to do so.

Our brains are constantly doing this for us, defining our reality when we do not have enough information to fully know our reality. I suggest here that our brains are also

leaving much of our actual reality out of our awareness as part of the same function.

So when this incomplete picture (see broken circle on left side in Figure 10) registers in our brains, we are frequently given a complete picture by our brains (as in closed circle on right side in Figure 10). In closing this circle, completing this incomplete picture for us, our brains are not showing us, *are not allowing us to know*, that the picture was actually incomplete, that there was actually information missing, and that various mechanisms and suggestions have been used to fill in the gaps.

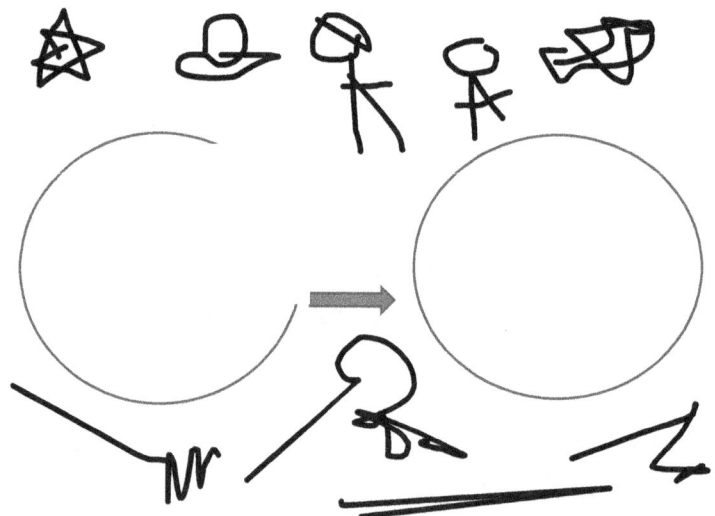

Figure 11:
Blocking Out Of Other Actual
(Or Perhaps Imagined) Information

BUT WHAT ABOUT
IMAGINATION?

Science suggests that the imagination process differs from the perception of reality process in that: although it is not fully determined (or determinable for that matter) where all or some imagined perceptions or imaginations originate in the brain, neural traces indicate that *imagined* images flow "down" from the parietal lobe to the occipital lobe.

A range of research considers the Human brain's differentiation between reality and imagination. In one area of study, researchers are finding that electrical activity in specific brain regions appears to *change direction* when study subjects are first asked to *imagine* a scene, and then are later asked to *watch* an actual video of that scene.

When the scene is being imagined, information flows "down" from the parietal lobe to the occipital lobe. (See Figure 12 regarding brain lobes.) Researchers call this "top-down" processing, with signals moving from a "higher-order" region of the brain to a "lower-order" region.

When the scene is being viewed on a video of that scene, signals are moving in the "opposite" direction, in a "bottom-up" processing with signals moving from a "lower-order" region of the brain to a "high-order" region of the brain.

What this indicates is that imagination (what I call *imagination function*) **and perception of reality (what I call** *reality function*) **originate in different regions of the brain.**

Here, I want to note that I at times add to these labels I give these functions so that these read:

imagination function/<u>illusion</u>
and
reality function/<u>illusion</u>

Note that above I add the term "illusion" to what I call the *imagination function*. What I describe as the *imagination function/illusion* tends to be readily accepted by many who read my work and or listen to my talks. However, when I then add the term "illusion" to what I call the *reality function*, describing the *reality function/**illusion**,* I get a range of responses, some confused, many doubting, some argumentative.

My first response is that, as always, I welcome the range of opinions regarding what I am presenting. My next response is that: what our brains tell us is our reality is also illusion, is simply what our brains have generated to depict as our reality, which is actually not our reality as there is always so much information missing.

The larger issue here is the way we accept what we are told we see, told we perceive, told we think, told we know. Our brains tell us to do so. ...

Herein, I am developing the notion that our brain has evolved to enforce our *<u>obedient unaware unquestioning buy-</u>*

_in_ to the definition of ourselves as only physical biological beings living in physical biological reality.

This buy-in holds us to a definition of ourselves that may be limiting our evolution and even our survival awarenesses and capabilities.

We must at least try on for size the expanded view offered on these pages, see where this exploration takes us. We must at least allow our imaginations to access this notion, this option, this expanded definition of our minds, and of our species, of who and what we actually are.

IMAGINATION
AS A
WORK AROUND TOOL

I continue to emphasize that we have only just begun to tap into the power of our imaginations to access further information about ourselves and our options--even about what we actually are, even about what we are told is real. Imagination may be a tool we very much need as we encounter augmenting survival pressures.

Our imaginations may allow us to work around our evolved-in brain programming dictating and perhaps limiting our realities and options.

Something about being able to imagine allows our brains and minds to _conceive of_ possibilities, options, and choices we can

make.[28] We can imagine what we are told is *not* there, and what we are *not* told *is* there. We can imagine possibilities we have not been allowed to consider or even to know about. We can imagine, just to explore, what we are told is not proven reality. **We can imagine a partial or entire reality that may or may not exist.**

This does *not* mean we can just "make stuff up" and tell ourselves it is real. This *does* mean we can use our imagination function to explore ideas and mental pathways that may otherwise be closed to us.

This brings me to a question I ask again and again: *can't our brains also be defining a reality for us that does not entirely exist or exist at all for that matter?* Simply because scientific studies are telling us messages moving up the brain determine reality and those moving down the brain determine imagined material, not reality, *does this ensure us that what our brains tell us is real is real?*

TIME TO VALUE IMAGINATION

Now, at first when we think of the value (whatever "value" implies to us) of Human Imagination, what may come to

---

[28] Of course, we must be careful to understand imagination the way I use it here. What I refer to herein is not an imagination that is fooling oneself into believing something. Instead, the *imagination function* I develop here is what I see as an *exploratory function* that our minds/brains, or our awareness-es, can use to find new avenues of knowing, develop new functions within themselves.

mind are movies, novels, comic books, stories, various uses of what we call artistic design, or story, or fiction of some form that "entertains" us.

Clearly the imagination can be a great thing, a great tool. Most Readers have used their imaginations in some way. Most Readers have explored their imaginations, at least to some extent. Most Readers have noticed that what the mind can *imagine* is virtually unlimited.

What we may not have realized (or been allowed to realize) is the great survival value of our imagination function (when it is healthy and not being manipulated, interfered or tampered with). Think of the consciousness as being as boundless as the imagination.

Think of the consciousness as using the *imagination exploration function* when needed, opening the brain and mind to expansions of awareness and possibility. Imagination can serve as a powerful tool.

Where we can consciously, via our awareness, take our minds (in safe healthy ways), is where we can in some form take ourselves.

Once we realize that our *selves* are not our bodies, we can travel (via our consciousness, its awareness, its focus) beyond where our physical bodies can take us. We can SEE BEYOND

OUR biological brain's LINE OF SIGHT.[29]

This will of course take a little re-learning of who we are, but we CAN do this. We have already started this realization, and now let's **consciously, purposefully, realize more**.

This is **not** to suggest that we create a fantasy and live within it to fool ourselves about the realities of our physical life and environment. This is **not** to suggest that we distract ourselves from pressing physical plane survival matters by wandering into seemingly "imaginary" realms and lingering there as a sort of avoidance tactic or distraction, or as flat out denial.

Such avoidance behavior is counter-survival. *In fact, as I indicate later in this book, and then continue to explain in the following book where I discuss certain brain "functions," we may even be programmed to behave in ...*

**reality-avoidant,
even counter-survival ways.**

This **is** to suggest that we **can** realize in full the potential and power of the Human Consciousness, that we can further evolve the Human Consciousness as we know it even while living here on Earth in biological Human Bodies.

---

[29] Refer again to *Volume 10* in this series, *SEEING BEYOND OUR LINE OF SIGHT*.

OUR CONSCIOUSNESS
CAN EVOLVE ITSELF

Several of the books in this *KEYS TO CONSCIOUSNESS AND SURVIVAL SERIES* raise a question regarding whether we must remain tied only to our biology to develop our life form of consciousness, to further evolve ourselves as the Species of Consciousness I suggest that we actually are.

As we look at this matter ever more closely, a truth unveils itself to us: Whether our consciousness *arose from* our biological brain, or our consciousness *existed before* our biological brain appeared and evolved, we can now let our consciousness further define itself as existing, further learning to exist, independent of our biological brain ...

**so as not to be
confined
exclusively to
physicality.**

**We can build upon
the complexity we have
already evolved or had
designed into us in some other way,
to extend ourselves,
our minds,
our consciousness-es
inter-dimensionally.**

This allows our consciousness freedom and option to move as it chooses, even to move itself (its imagination, its awareness, its center or point of focus) in and out of physicality.

When and if needed, we can even be free of the restriction to physicality that biology requires. We can expand into a greater range of existence for survival purposes, if necessary.[30]

Our Human Consciousness has so many advanced capabilities still to be recognized (or remembered) and *activated*. We can reach beyond the confines of our biological physicality, the confines our biological brains hold us within, to gain access to new dimensions of our SELVES.

We can unveil the *hidden interdimensional awareness instinct* we carry deep within.

**It is time now,
time to listen to deeply embedded instinct....**

**We can develop
ever greater access to
our expansive
interdimensional awareness and capabilities,
and access this ESSENTIAL access,
this KEY awareness function....**

---

[30] See *Volume 3* in this series, titled, *UNVEILING THE HIDDEN INSTINCT: UNDERSTANDING OUR INTERDIMENSIONAL SURVIVAL AWARENESS.*

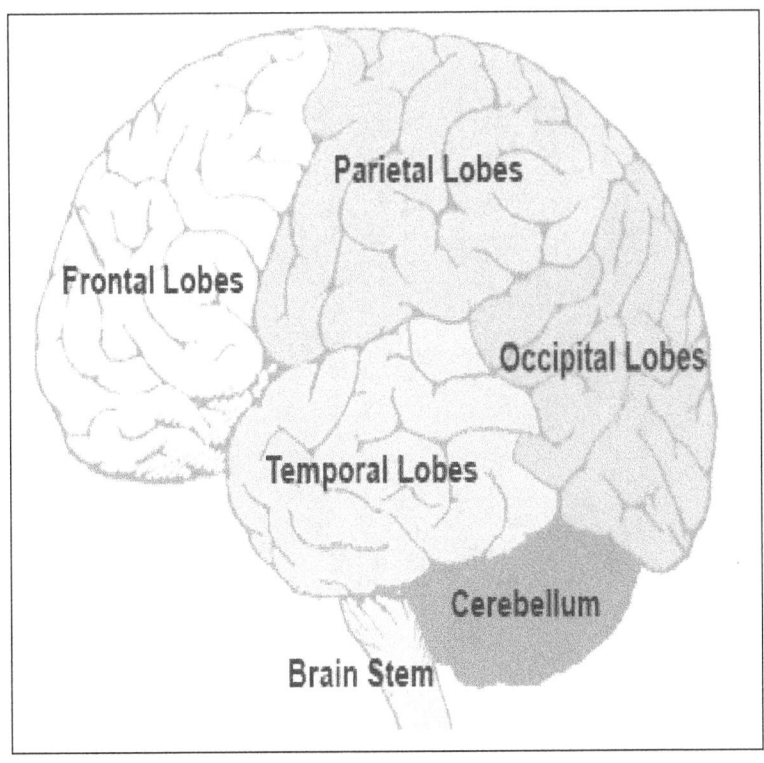

Figure 12: Diagram of Brain's Lobes
Courtesy of Australian gov.au

αΩα

6

WE CAN EVOLVE OUR AWARE CONSCIOUSNESS, BUT ARE WE PROGRAMMED NOT TO KNOW THIS?

We can see that, at least so far, our brain, mind (and consciousness *if* this consciousness is indeed arising from our biological brain), have developed and or evolved without our having much say in the process or direction of this evolution. Somehow, we Earth Humans signed onto, or were produced by, *an evolutionary process that we have had relatively little say in.*

We cannot say whether or not we have arrived in this situation by outside direction or interference. However, we can see that we have not directed our own evolution, nor our own genetic coding, nor our own brain wiring.

We may now begin to at least wonder about this possibility: Perhaps we have been subjected to a *random* evolutionary process or experiment (asking, what species can survive with what traits), or perhaps we have been *subjects* in some other perhaps higher intelligence's process or experiment (e.g., which species if any can survive this extinction scenario).

OUR THEORIES REGARDING
OUR CONSCIOUSNESS

Humans have developed many different theories regarding the Human Consciousness. Some perspectives do of course tell us that the Human Consciousness has evolved through several levels during the biological evolution of the Human Brain. For example, some researchers tell us that there is a basic "sensori-motor" consciousness in "lower level" animals who do not have the particular verbal skills Humans have.

This thinking says that the "lower level consciousness" is distinguished from the "higher order consciousness" that Humans are said to have "evolved." It is argued that during evolution, biological brain functions that generate a higher order consciousness were "selected for" (as per the survival of the fittest species theory of evolution) and thus emerged as the Human Brain evolved to its present form.

To take this to its simple extreme, this view says that our evolution moved us in the direction of having an ever "higher" consciousness (apparently higher than it was earlier in our evolution).

From within its own world view, this biological theory of the evolution of our *biological* consciousness makes sense, *at least to some extent.* (See Figure 9.) To develop or evolve the obviously extensive and complex characteristics of Human Beings, some sort of "natural" or "natural selection" process

likely tried out components and then selected for what made Human Beings what they are today. Thus, how we are today can be attributed to our evolution, *or so we are told*.

Can this line of thinking be implying that other animals' consciousness-es were not selected for (in terms of modern planetary eco-niche dominance), were perhaps even selected *out* of dominance, by a natural process that allowed Humans to evolve their consciousness to "higher" levels, and with this, their dominance of Earth's biosphere to emerge more powerful, and perhaps even more destructive, day by day???

What evolution scenario would be designed this way?

This thinking again links biological evolution with the development of consciousness. Yes, I generally sense that the Human Consciousness we presently see among biological Humans living on Earth is likely a more complex and individuated consciousness than that of a banana slug. (Apparently there is a value placed on having what claims to be a more complex consciousness. We, of course, are told by our brains that this is the case.)

Nevertheless, I sometimes ask whether the more complex consciousness obscures itself by its own complexity. Hence, toward a clearer understanding of our present situation, I add as per my discussion in this book, that:

1)

The evolution (or even possibly re-evolution) of Earth Human Consciousness and Mind is still in process;

2)

There can be further advancements or developments in our Human Consciousness;

3)

The Human evolving here on Earth can reach into its Human Evolution and consciously advance itself, and even form major next steps (LEAPS) in the evolution of itself as a species of consciousness, the Human Consciousness;

4)

The Human Consciousness need not be capped or stopped here where it is presently, with the capabilities it presently has (or perceives it has);

5)

Factors limiting the evolution of the Human Mind and even of its Human Brain have been placed within our genetic code either by random evolutionary effects, or perhaps by some intervening process such as a directing, or designing, and or implanting process;

6)

We Humans here on Earth can detect and then consciously reach beyond those limiting factors;

7)

We Humans here on Earth can break free of limits that have been placed upon us by random evolution or by intervening factors;

8)

We Humans can take control of our own evolution and can evolve our SELVES to new levels of awareness and consciousness;

9)

We Humans can bring new capabilities to our consciousness, capabilities that are key to our survival;

10)

We Humans may not be the only species doing all the above.

WHERE DID CONSCIOUSNESS COME FROM?

As diagrammed in Figure 13, the range of evolutionary, biological, theories regarding the arising of Human Consciousness includes several explanations for how this thing we call "higher" consciousness came to be a characteristic of some life forms such as ours.

Again, note that the *emergence* of consciousness is often explained as a *trend* in the biological evolution of all life.

Yes, it is argued by some that the Human Consciousness has been selected for, that the species that can dominate the present Earth niche has this Human Consciousness. Hence the *development of (**and perhaps dominance by**)* Earth Human Consciousness is often explained as a series of processes within this biological evolutionary trend here in this Earth niche.

HOW NATURAL
HAS NATURAL SELECTION BEEN?

Whether or not the basic "natural" selection that some Earth-based evolutionary scientists teach us about has truly been the (or a) primary **functional operant** of our biological evolution until now, I say we can consciously create a new functional operant to work on our evolutionary process. *We ourselves can consciously be the* **functional operant** *at work in our own evolutionary process.*

By *functional operant,* I suggest that being consciously aware of, and then involved in, engaged in, even directing, our own evolution is being *functionally operant.* What would this look like? Can our biological brain allow us to imagine this as it would be on a grand scale, a species wide, even a biosphere scale?

Sure, we already believe we are already "making a difference" and "doing our part" in moving Human behavior to new levels of power and of morality, and of desirability. **However, the species level awareness I am envisioning here**

may require ACTIVATION OF KEYS buried deep within our own consciousness. These KEYS may unlock the door to our own full and free access to our own CONTINUUM OF CONSCIOUSNESS. (See again another book in this series for definition of this continuum: *SEEING BEYOND OUR LINE OF SIGHT.*)

So, of course we can be *actively operational,* turn our awareness to what being *functionally operant* can be. And, we surely have a right to be our own *operant within our own evolution.*

Why would we, as a life form who is conscious of itself, consciously choose to have our evolution operated by an invisible or outside factor, or by a random factor such as a natural selection or a natural accident?

This was not a conscious choice we, our species, made. We have not consciously chosen for ourselves an extinction scenario based upon our believing we are primarily biological beings who may become biologically extinct— with no other routes to survival.

→PERCEIVED TRENDS IN <u>BIOLOGICAL</u> EVOLUTION→ (APPARENTLY) LEADING TO "EMERGENCE" OF CONSCIOUS LIFE AND CONSCIOUSNESS

matter → → life

physical living → → "conscious" living

- -

→<u>PERCEIVED INCREASING SURVIVAL VALUE TRENDS</u>→ IN "DEVELOPING" AND ADVANCING <u>BIOLOGICAL</u> CONSCIOUSNESS IN <u>BIOLOGICAL</u> EVOLUTION

presumed survival value low	→ → →	presumed survival value high
unconscious collective consciousness	→ → →	self aware individual consciousness
"lower order" consciousness	→ → →	"higher order" consciousness
"simple" consciousness	→ →. →	"complex" consciousness
"basic brain" and its consciousness	→ → →	"advanced brain" and its consciousness

Figure 13:
Perceived Trends In Our Biological Evolution

αΩα

7
IF WE WISH TO SURVIVE

If the present state of Human Consciousness is indeed the product of some kind of *biological evolutionary* natural selection, and if this natural selection now risks *(or is even perhaps designed to risk)* our species becoming extinct, might we want to take over the process of our own evolution? Might we want to decide for ourselves whether or not we become extinct?

Yes, if we wish to survive.

Being alert to threats to our survival is essential, yes. Of course, many say we are already alert to survival, primarily in the form of environmental matters, and taking action. And yes, we are.

Yet, while the work of many Humans living in this biosphere to help protect this biosphere and life within it is so hugely important, even essential, this book is also looking at a still larger matter: *the possibility that we Humans are in the biospheric stress situation we are in for more than our own accidental or negligence or carelessness reasons.*

What am I asking is...

Could there be more going on here? If Earth based biological selection processes are indeed *tuned* to some oddly defined survival of the seeming fittest, then the fittest species (which can and may likely include more than Humans of course) may want to now choose to have the understandings offered in this book. This may require our detecting any possible *extinction scenario* that may be being naturally or otherwise tested on us by something/s or someone/s we cannot quite detect.

EVEN THE
SEEMING FITTEST SPECIES

MAY HAVE TO INTERCEDE TO

OVERRIDE
ITS OWN
EXTINCTION.

Survival may require us to see more of our reality, perhaps even allow for the possibility that we are some sort of **test species** *in some kind of* **extinction experiment,** *in some sort of* **species extinction trial.**

If we do sense this, we must intercede to override the metaphorical and or actual **experimental protocol of the intelligent designers** *experimenting on us. We can then strive to break out of what we see of this protocol-driven scenario. (Consider Figure 15 later in this book, "Are We Subjects in an Extinction Experiment?)*

Survival may require the seemingly so-called fittest species to have the awareness and the conscious ability to take conscious control of its own evolution, to **take conscious control even of the evolution of its own consciousness.** *We, the Human Species, can be a species who does this. (We may be one of several species on Earth and beyond so doing.)*

There can be those among us who do see this option. We can go ahead and develop the awareness of this form of deeply heightened and highly aware consciousness reaching beyond the limitations of our biological brain.

As we do so, the numbers of those of us engaged in further evolving both our biologically-based and our non-biologically-based species consciousness to the **species survival level** *may grow. We can then reach critical mass of our species, achieve a* **critical mass of awareness,** *in order to evolve our species so that we all (or at least those who wish to participate in this process) can consciously seek to consciously survive in applying this extended awareness of ourselves as a species of consciousness.*

NOT ONLY BIOLOGICAL
EVOLUTION....

Of course, we are not necessarily entirely tied to our biological evolution, and in fact this is one of the keys to the discussion this book offers. I say we have consciousness-es that can choose to override biological evolution, and even generate for themselves their own evolution.

Whatever path our consciousness-es have followed to get to this point, our consciousness-es can break free and take on a self-determining, self-evolving, independence of their own.

This may mean overriding any exclusive control of us by only our biological brain, and thus by only our biology. Of course we can continue to live in physicality with biological vehicles/bodies, as long as we can and or choose to, however we can realize we are not only our biological vehicles/bodies that our biological brains tell us we are.

We are living here in this biological Earth niche. Here, our **self-evolving as a species of consciousness** can mean that we evolve the capability to choose to stay within, or to depart from, and or to come and go from, the confines that biological evolution has placed upon our consciousness and therefore upon us. Recognizing these confines, their defining coding and wiring implemented primarily via our biological brain, is essential.

We of course, can choose to live only within the dictates of these biologically-defined confines. This is of course our choice, a choice our brain is generally making for us whether or not we are making this choice for ourselves.

Or we can choose to SEE BEYOND these confines, to SEE BEYOND OUR LINE OF SIGHT, to look past the dictates and parameters of the reality defined for us by our biological

brain.[31] This looking beyond, seeing beyond, does not mean we die or disappear. Simply because we expand the realm of our consciousness does not mean we cease physically existing. Nor does this mean we leave our biological bodies.

This means we develop a *conscious choice in the matter* of where we wish to be when, where we wish to focus ourselves when, where we wish to move the center of our consciousness-es to and from, into and out of, how we wish to expand ourselves into territories where we already do live.

We can learn to travel via our consciousness-es to be where we need to locate, to center, to focus, our consciousness-es in order to survive.

We can evolve ourselves to utilize what is buried deep within us: our full consciousness and its full capabilities.

(NOTE: See figures and chapters in this and also the following book, *OVERRIDING THE EXTINCTION SCENARIO*, Part <u>Two</u>, regarding the potential of our Human Brain to further evolve itself, as a vehicle for our greater *conscious access to our own consciousness, the place where we already do exist.*[32])

---

[31] Again refer to *Volume 10* in this series, *SEEING BEYOND OUR LINE OF SIGHT.*

[32] As I explain in this book, *OVERRIDING THE EXTINCTION SCENARIO, Part One*, and further in other books in this *KEYS TO CONSCIOUSNESS AND SURVIVAL SERIES* such as, *HOW TO DIE AND SURVIVE*, and *UNVEILING THE HIDDEN INSTINCT*, and in the related *ADVANCING AWARENESS EXERCISES* contained in those books, I view the awareness

In moving forward now, we will want to ask again and again central questions such as these:

- Is the Human Consciousness part of a larger species of Humanity, of consciousness, or even of a higher cosmic level consciousness?

- Was our consciousness out there in the cosmos prior to our biological evolution?
  If so, whose consciousness was this? Ours?

- Did our consciousness come into, or perhaps become trapped in, limited by, physical dimensions and physical bodies?

Readers will have various perspectives on the above and other debated issues. And this is alright, this is welcome. Any viewpoint can still attend to the matter of survival of the Human Species beyond what it has so far envisioned for itself here on Earth and also perhaps beyond.

Still, no matter how natural so-called "natural" selection is said to have been, no matter how purely biological and even random evolution here on Earth may or may not have been, no matter where our Human Consciousness may or may not have come from …

---

function of our brains (and minds) as the **operant arm** of our consciousness. Hence, advancing awareness increases conscious access to the consciousness itself.

...we Humans can step up now and have a major say in what happens next. [This *step up* is the METAXIS LEAP *(Metaxis-- Light Energy Action Process for conscious evolution)* concept I define in other of my writings.[33]]

LIMITS OF
VARIOUS PRACTICES

Throughout their history here on Earth, Human Beings have wanted access to their own and other higher consciousness-es, even to their Gods. Various religious and philosophical programs, practices, and rituals seek and offer advancements in the capabilities of the consciousness. Indeed, the powers of belief, of intense focus, of specific practices such as prayer and meditation, are offered. Also offered are practices aimed specifically at generating "altered states," frequently telling participants that altered states are themselves the pathways to their higher consciousness-es.

These and other practices can be profoundly, generally, or at least somewhat useful to various people, while confusing or even at times harmful to others. Unfortunately, too many who call themselves leaders, guides, even shamans, do not know in depth: the functioning of the Human mind and brain; and or exactly what they are teaching; and or have other agendas, despite their claims to the contrary. (When

---

[33] See *Volume 3* in this series, *UNVEILING THE HIDDEN INSTINCT: UNDERSTANDING OUR INTERDIMENSIONAL SURVIVAL AWARE-NESS.* See also *Volume 4,* titled, *HOW TO DIE AND SURVIVE.* See also *Volume 10,* titled, *SEEING BEYOND OUR LINE OF SIGHT.* Refer to reading list at the end of this present book.

various methods of working with people and their minds and brains – such as hypnosis, and EMDR, for example -- actually are producing actual brain changes, the responsibility for reaching into these minds and brains is significant. Yet, too many take this reaching in far too lightly.)

What is quite interesting is that the altered states being generated by various approaches are offering just that, *altered* states. What I am saying in this book is that we Humans living on Earth are likely living day to day in an already altered state that prevents us from full access to ourselves, as our brains are programmed not to have direct access to the Human state of consciousness we already do have. (I say more, in later chapters of this and the following book, about how our own biological brains are programmed to block out essential information and essential levels of awareness.)

However, I am suggesting that now we can actually break free of limits imposed on the evolution of our earthly biology-based Human Consciousness. We can do so by digging far deeper into ourselves, our behaviors, our programming, even into our own awareness of the presence of our coding. We can dig right down into our own coding to see what may require rewiring or even overriding.

We can see that we have been wired, programmed, genetically coded. We can find both natural (evolutionary or even accidental) and perhaps also implanted blocks to our own biological (and other) evolution and awareness.

Then we can consciously evolve means of releasing these blocks and trapping patterns when these are problematic, even dangerous, threats to survival.[34] We can free ourselves of *evolutionary limits* in order to survive. Our consciousness-es do have the capacity for this. (See the following book, *OVERRIDING THE EXTINCTION SCENARIO, Part Two,* for further definition of, and a deeper look at, *implanted evolutionary limits.*)

WE CAN
REVOLT

We can revolt against any implanted locks capping us, placing an implanted *ceiling on our evolution.* We can do this by consciously adapting, by consciously evolving, *our core life form, **our awareness**, our **aware consciousness**, which is who we actually are.*[35]

We can center ourselves, our core life form, center who we are, in our *focal center.* And then, we can hold this focal center

---

[34] Refer to *Volume 6* of this *KEYS TO CONSCIOUSNESS AND SURVIVAL SERIES,* titled, *OVERRIDING THE EXTINCTION SCENARIO, Part Two,* and also *Volume 10* of this series, titled, *SEEING BEYOND OUR LINE OF SIGHT.* And, see books in the *FACES OF ADDICTION SERIES,* also by Dr. Angela Brownemiller, such as *SEEING THE HIDDEN FACE OF ADDICTION.* These and other books are listed in the reading list at the end of this present book.

[35] See definition and discussion of *our aware consciousness* in *Volume 3* in this *KEYS TO CONSCIOUSNESS AND SURVIVAL SERIES,* titled, *UNVEILING THE HIDDEN INTINCT: UNDERSTANDING OUR INTERDIMENSIONAL SURVIVAL AWARENESS.*

of ours in whatever of our own physical and nonphysical bodies we choose to call our location. We can determine for ourselves the *center of our consciousness,* of our true identity. We can choose for ourselves where we want to be along our own ***continuum of consciousness.***[36]

This Human Consciousness is vast and its actual vastness as yet unrealized by many Humans living on Earth in physical bodies. We must ask whether perhaps the Human Species has been separated from its expansive self, and from its full survival awareness-es and capabilities, separated from itSELF ***by its very controlling biologically evolved physical brain.*** And we must ask, how might ***this separation have come into, or have been placed into, us as biological Humans?***

We must allow ourselves to ask whether our biological evolution may have "advanced" our biological bodies and brains while, at the same time, **devolved** our access to ourselves, to our true life form, to the vast capabilities of our Human Species of Consciousness. *DE-evolution is not evolution, although we may be programmed to believe it is.*

Again, we have to at least ask: Could our evolution be merely the product of random natural selection, or could our evolution perhaps be someone else's extinction scenario experiment?

---

[36] See definition and discussion of our ***continuum of consciousness*** in *Volume 10* in this series, titled *SEEING BEYOND OUR LINE OF SIGHT.*

KNOWING
OUR OWN CONSCIOUSNESS

Many of us living here on Earth do already to some extent understand and appreciate the true, expansive, and potentially enduring nature of our Human Consciousness. We walk around with our consciousness every day, we live with our consciousness, we sometimes even think about our consciousness.

But how well do we know this consciousness of ours? And how well do we know the consciousness of our species? *How aware is our consciousness?*

This thing we call Humanity is more than a behavior or an attitude. This is the precious essence of who we are. This *is* who we are. We are the Species of the Human Consciousness.

Humanity itself is an essence, a consciousness. The species of Human Consciousness can detect itself as itself, and then can activate itself to be who it actually is:

**a species traveling in
physical plane 3-D Earth via physical bodies,
a biologized species for now.**

As a consciousness, Humanity can be its chosen level of alertness, focus, clarity, and *awareness.* However, these descriptors hardly capture the absolute depth and power of these aspects of ourselves, of who/what Humanity actually is.

We are a species of consciousness.

The Human Consciousness
itself
is our life form.

PATH OF CONSCIOUSNESS: CHART

If we are in essence our consciousness,
how did we get to be a consciousness?
Is this a path of Human Consciousness
diverging from biological evolution?

Fully Independent Consciousness (h)
Consciousness beyond Brain (g)
Some Consciousness beyond Brain (f)
****Biological Brain with Consciousness (e)*
Biological Brain with "a" Consciousness (d)
Developed Biological Brain (c)
"Simple" Biological Brain (b)
Biological Life (a)

So, did our consciousness suddenly appear
        in the brain of the Biological Human***?
Did consciousness just drop into our biological life form***?
Or did an evolution of our brain toward and into consciousness
                                        actually take place?
Did this evolution actually proceed from:
(a) biological life, to
(b) biological life with a "simple" brain, to
(c) biological life with a more "developed" biological brain, to
(d) biological life/brain with at least "a" consciousness of some sort, to
(e) biological brain with (what we assume to be) *our* consciousness***?
And can it be that this consciousness, however it formed,
can further evolve/move into...
        (f) some existence (seemingly) outside of the biological brain, to
        (g) existence with or without the biological brain, to
        (h) fully independent consciousness
                        diverged from any biological constraints....

Figure 14:
Path of Consciousness Chart

αΩα

8
THE VOICE OF
OUR HIGHER CONSCIOUSNESS
IS CALLING

It is quite possible that Humanity is a life form that has traveled far longer and far more than we are allowed to realize, than our biological brains may allow us to know, to perceive, to remember. It is quite possible we have traveled throughout the physical plane and beyond, throughout the interdimensional cosmos.

We have perhaps traveled as a vagabond *species of consciousness* that has been displaced several times by various forces seeking to stop it, block it, even end it.

Now, we Humans are alerting ourselves to what is and has been happening to us here on Earth, in our 3-D biologized form.

Listen, deep within our hearts and minds, we can hear Humanity calling. We are calling ourselves ... the higher levels of ourselves, of our species, are calling us. This calling is our Human Consciousness, who we Humans truly are. This call is well underway.

We have been sensing these higher signals from our higher consciousness—from the heart of our *species of consciousness*—from the force of Humanity itself. We have been sending this call to ourselves for quite some time. And now, it is time for us to recognize in full what it is that we have been feeling and hearing, sensing.

Listen, feel this, sense this, know this: Our awareness of this signal is rising. It is important we understand what we are hearing, so that we can respond in positive ways rather than with misinterpretation, confusion, anxiety, fear, and chaos. Protective and proactive survival awareness (rather than blinding fear and anxiety) is essential here.

Our actual survival quite possibly depends on this.

VOICE OF HIGHER HUMANITY

For a moment, or for longer if you like, realize that you are already here and that you already hear this call. You are already letting your mind's ears open to hear these sounds coming in like waves of energy and light, to feel this energy of ourselves, of our higher selves.

This is our consciousness speaking to us. This is who we truly are contacting our SELVES.

Absorb this beautiful uniquely woven voice, the voice of our consciousness, of our higher Humanity, singing to us from

across the universe, from around the cosmos, calling to worlds everywhere, singing of Humanity's presence here and through time.

This voice is who brings Humanity itself to its very awareness of itself. This voice is who calls we Humans to the heights of ourselves. This voice is who reveals to us our vast potential. This voice suggests how vast our reach into this cosmos can be, has already been in other epochs elsewhere, and already is. This voice is our voice, the voice of the **Cosmic Species of Humanity**, the Human Species of Consciousness we actually are.

If you wish to, you can hear this voice, you can feel this voice, you can be this voice. This is our voice, this is your voice. This is all of us, this is you. This is our Humanity. This is your Humanity. And this Humanity is a precious element in this grand cosmos.

Listen to yourself, to us.
Welcome home.

PRECIOUS
HUMANITY

Humanity is a precious gem, a unique element, a rare force in this universe and in this cosmos. Humanity is a force, a life force, that has yet to be entirely activated (or re-activated) by the members of this physicalized Biological Human Species here on Earth.

Let's pause to consider this possibility, this imaginary scenario:

Perhaps Humanity itself brought Humans here to this planet, Earth. Humanity fueled, materialized, and then biologized the descension of itself, of its species, into this 3-D physical plane on Earth. This was done by Humanity to protect Humanity for a time, to give Humanity shelter in a physical habitat.

However, perhaps like a window being cleaned, or one's vision being corrected, we are just beginning to see what has happened. It is becoming more and more clear to us that Humanity's effort to find shelter in 3-D was perhaps intercepted, even hijacked. Little did Humanity see coming the interceding by other forces and factors, other intelligences, into this process, the tampering with the biological evolution process of Human Beings on Earth.

Perhaps opportunistic intelligences did seek control of the physical-ization and subsequent physical, biological, (then even socio-cultural), evolution of Humanity, for their own purposes. Their own purposes may indeed be what I call the **extinction trials in which various species** *such as ourselves* **are tested for their viability in various niches and settings**. *(Figure 19 explores this scenario.)*

Physicalized, biologized, Humans on 3-D physical plane Earth call themselves Human Beings, frequently not seeing

that they may be but one form of the Human Life Form and its Human Life Force. Yet, we Humans must now see this, and must bring our full range of capabilities to our own attention, in order to survive what is happening to us in the physical plane and beyond.

WE CAN SURVIVE BY
KNOWING

We Humans can survive by knowing who we truly are, by being who we truly are. Humanity need not be extinguished, ever. Humanity can endure the test of time and space, as well as other tests and pressures such as survival pressures, and even extinction trials to which we may be being subjected (or may be subjecting ourselves).

Humanity can now consciously step up to detect and surpass the implanted, programmed-in **evolutionary blocks** that seek to halt our progress, to stop our freeing ourselves.

These blocks have, by one or more means, been randomly, accidentally, and or purposefully programmed into, implanted into, evolved into, our genetic coding. These blocks do control us, hold us back, may even weaken our ability to *rapidly adapt* to shifting (physical plane as well as interdimensional) environments.

And all our environments are in essence interdimensional, as we are indeed interdimensional beings, a *lifeform of consciousness*. Perhaps these blocks are actually blocking us

from fully accessing our *interdimensional SELVES,* and the *essential awareness-es these interdimensional SELVES carry.*

Understanding who we truly are means that:

(a) we Earth Humans may be able to discover ways to adapt more rapidly to shifting environmental and other pressures; and,

(b) we may be able to better understand our options for and various means of consciously surviving along our own *continuum of consciousness.*

We have the capabilities to do this, and we must access these capabilities in full now. We must. This means we must understand we are not only a physical biological life form. We are a species already living along our own **continuum of consciousness.**[37]

KEY IN
THIS SURVIVAL

KEY in this survival is our knowing who we truly are: We are citizens of the cosmos.

We ourselves are interdimensional beings. We are actually a species of consciousness. We live along our personal and

---

[37] Again see other books in this series for definition of this **continuum of consciousness** where we actually do live. Begin with *Volume 10* titled, *SEEING BEYOND OUR LINE OF SIGHT.*

species CONTINUUM OF CONSCIOUSNESS.[38]

Humanity can adapt and thus preserve its true mobility, its ability to travel to and from, and live even concurrently within, niches here in physical plane 3-D as well as in other dimensions of our consciousness.

These interdimensional niches exist within our consciousness, along our continuum of consciousness.

These niches are our domains, domains that we can conceive of, that we do already live in, and that are ours to inhabit.

This is a matter of our ever further understanding and ever further accessing the power of our awareness, and the power of our increasing awareness of our consciousness. This is a matter of asking our biological brain why this access is restricted, what can be done to remove this restriction. Or, perhaps this is a matter of understanding that while the biological brain may restrict access, we can nevertheless access ourselves independently of this biological brain.

Humanity itself can discover, access, and apply the *multidimensional capabilities of its consciousness* to save itself-- perhaps even to help heal the biological Earth biosphere niche.

---

[38] See other books in this *KEYS TO CONSCIOUSNESS AND SURVIVAL SERIES* for definition and discussion of this **CONTINUUM OF CONSCIOUSNESS**, most specifically see *Volume 10* titled, *SEEING BEYOND OUR LINE OF SIGHT*. See also *Volume 3* titled, *UNVEILING THE HIDDEN INSTINCT*.

Please note that Humanity must speak to its Earth-based physicalized Human Beings now, must speak expressly to Humans living on Earth now. Humanity, your highest essence, needs you, calls you.

Yes, where some form of diminishment of the nature and power of Humanity has come into play here on Earth, in this physical dimension, our (re-) expanding our awareness can correct this trend and protect against it.

Awaking our operant arm, our aware consciousness,[39] is key to our further activating our consciousness as a life form and as a survival power.[40]

Reclaiming ourselves as beings who live along our own and our species' continuum of consciousness is KEY in our survival.[41]

---

[39] Although terms/phrases such as "what we are *conscious of*" and "being *conscious of*" are commonly used, are even popular jargon, these overlap with discussions of our consciousness and or of what is frequently called "higher" consciousness. Hence, for more clarity, I define and use the phrase *aware consciousness* when I am referring to what we are actually aware of, noting the large body of our consciousness we also carry, or have some access to, yet are not fully aware of. I view our awareness as the *operant arm* of our consciousness, as being our *access to our consciousness*.

[40] See the **awareness activation exercises** in *Volume 3*, titled *UNVEILING THE HIDDEN INSTINCT*, and also in *Volume 4*, titled *HOW TO DIE AND SURVIVE*. Refer to reading list at end of this present book.

[41] Again, see *Volume 10* in this series, titled *SEEING BEYOND OUR LINE OF SIGHT*, for definition of this CONTINUUM OF CONSCIOUSNESS.

αΩα

9
DETECTING
OURSELVES AS
SUBJECTS IN
EXTINCTION TRIALS

If physicalized, biologized, Humanity has been interfered with, blocked from its actual awareness of its full interdimensional nature, it is time we detect this. It is time we recognize what implanted or accidental obstacles are presently blocking our full access to our own *continuum of consciousness*, where we already do live.

As implausible as the possibility of outside interference, of such *evolutionary tampering*, may sound, as overwhelming as this realization may be for those of us living our every day lives as best we can, it may be time for us to step up to this realization—or at least to examine this possibility and its ramifications. Let's continue to do this here....

IF HUMANITY
HAS BEEN
DESIGNED AND CONFINED

As a *species of consciousness*, it is our physical biology, our physicalized Humanity, that has somehow held itself back or

been held back from particular essential survival awareness-es, options, and capabilities, stopped from progressing, even perhaps purposively...

detoured

devolved

by evolutionary interference forces —

by particular

intelligent designers and experimenters —

by interdimensional captors.

Physicalized Humanity may have been restrained and contained here on this 3-D Earth plane, so as to hold Humanity itself under some form of control or what I define (in the following book) as an **EVOLUTIONARY CEILING**.[42] This ceiling may be implanted to keep physicalized Humanity from its full potential, to trap it in third dimensional confines, to ensure that it forgets or does not access its full interdimensional potential, its actual nature.[43]

In my years working with and analyzing the Human Mind, I have detected what I will describe here as the presence of an ...

---

[42] See *Volume 6* in this series, which is the following book, *OVERRIDING THE EXTINCTION SCENARIO, Part Two,* for my definition and discussion of this EVOLUTIONARY CEILING and of the EVOLUTIONARY BLOCK this ceiling places upon us.

[43] See again further discussion of this in *Volume 3,* titled *UNVEILING THE HIDDEN INSTINCT: UNDERSTANDING OUR INTERDIMENSIONAL SURVIVAL AWARENESS.*

evolutionary block.

I suggest that part of the **evolutionary block** implanted into the Earth Human coding (genetic coding that directs the wiring of the biological Human Brain) is a **block on our ability to fully conceive of our non-biological aspects**. This is a block on our ability to know we can develop this already present inter-dimensional aspect of ourselves.

This is a block on our fully accessing our ability to, on an as needed basis, locate within our interdimensional niches, niches which are already domains of our own consciousness. This understanding of our locating this way involves our recognizing our capacity to migrate to and from, to *trans*migrate to and from, 3-D physical biological as well as *interdimensional niches (domains of our own consciousness)* we may have to travel to and from to survive.[44]

Note that what is biological about us and our brains is wonderful and wondrous. Nothing here says to abandon this aspect of ourselves while living here in our physical bodies.

However, it is important to see that what is biological about *what our biological brains allow us to know about ourselves* is in

---

[44] See the definition and discussion of this TRANSMIGRATION in *Volume 3* in this series, titled, *UNVEILING THE HIDDEN INSTINCT: UNDERSTANDING OUR INTERDIMENSIONAL SURVIVAL AWARE-NESS.*

essence, BIO and LOGICAL. It is logical for our biological coding to omit or perhaps even deny our own access to our own interdimensional niches. Non-biological domains are in essence not logical or allowed to be fully logical from a bio-LOGICAL standpoint.

TRAVEL TO,
ACCESS TO,
OUR NICHES

By *travel to*, in terms of interdimensional niches, herein I am not referring to physical travel, rather to a very basic *movement or shift of awareness*, even a …

transmigration, of
the <u>focus</u>, of the <u>focal point, of our consciousness</u>
via its operant arm, its awareness.[45]

This is knowledge we may have once freely held. This knowledge is key to who we are. We have a right to access our knowledge, our consciousness of who we are.

Once we are aware of this…

---

[45] I have more fully developed this concept and described first steps of such "travel" in other books of this *KEYS TO CONSCIOUSNESS AND SURVIVAL SERIES*. See *Volume 3* titled, *UNVEILING THE HIDDEN INSTINCT: UNDERSTANDING OUR INTERDIMENSIONAL SURVIVAL AWARENESS*. See also *Volumes 4 and 5* in this series, titled, *HOW TO DIE AND SURVIVE*.

we can unveil
this instinct we carry so deeply within ourselves:
our interdimensional survival awareness.[46]

NOTE

Let's think for a moment about some examples of 3-D Human hierarchies. Recall times in Human Earth history where large sectors of the population were kept from learning to read, so as to keep them under control of the so-called "literate elite."

And, think of how some religions and groups have led people to believe that only so-called "chosen" or "special" ones, or only those deemed so-called "righteous" or "saved" people, can have access to what is then labeled "higher knowledge," "higher consciousness," even access to an "after" life of some form.

Of course, what these individuals were actually admitting to us was that their supposedly "higher" consciousness was not exactly advanced or higher, as advanced consciousness is likely by nature _inclusive,_ not exclusive in access.

EVOLUTION AFFECTED

The evolution of Humanity into this Earth biosphere has

---

[46] See again _Volume 3,_ titled _UNVEILING THE HIDDEN INSTINCT._

been deterred from its full potential. And, as explained in this book, this may have grave consequences for what may be the entire *interdimensional species* of **Humanity.**

However, we Humans can choose to see what is happening. And, we can know that Humanity has the capacity to free itself from confines not of its own making as well as from confines of its own making.

Humanity can free itself of any threats to its continued and full existence within and beyond this physical plane. Humanity can rightfully access its own *continuum of consciousness.*[47]

WE MUST RECOGNIZE OUR
INTERDIMENSIONAL MANIFEST

We Humans can most definitely survive. We Humans have this option. We Humans can fulfill our *interdimensional manifest*. We can be who we truly are. We can rise to the highest, purest, most fulfilled nature of our journey through space and time here on Earth and through this cosmos.

We can begin by recognizing the *expansive character* of true Human Nature, the true character of our actual Human

---

[47] Again note, this *continuum of consciousness* is defined and discussed in other books in this series such as, *SEEING BEYOND OUR LINE OF SIGHT.*

Essence, Humanity's Life Force.

We Humans can have an actual say in our actual future.

This is to say that the survival of the Human Species is to a great extent in our hands, or better stated, in our minds — in our consciousness-es. *Our survival is ours to define and to bring about for ourselves.*

We must be able to see what is going on here in order to deal with it. Again, this book presents an option I sense the Human Species may indeed have and must at least explore now...

We have undergone extensive biological development and or evolution here on physical plane Earth. It is time for us to understand, to be allowed to remember, we are a life form that can and does inhabit both physical and non-physical environments.

It is time for us to ever more consciously understand that we are a *species of consciousness* **living along our** *continuum of consciousness.* **This is our actual and far more expansive niche.**

For us to know this, to fully see this, we may have to remove the lock or block the programming operating our biological brain has on our full access to our full consciousness.

This is both a minor and a major leap in our evolution, in

the evolution of our awareness, and of the <u>mobility</u> of our awareness.

WE <u>CAN</u> MAKE THIS
LEAP

I say that we Humans have the capacity to make a great and conscious *leap in our evolution*, and that the time may come when we must indeed be able to rapidly make this leap.[48]

In fact, our own due diligence as a species who wishes to continue to survive requires us to know of, and to be able to directly apply and to directly utilize, our actual consciousness, our interdimensional mind and its higher level transit and transformative, even *transmigrational*, capabilities.

I have no desire to make this material so far out that it turns away Readers who will not join me despite my extensive research, training, and professional qualifications. I therefore present what I am saying herein as simply and clearly as possible; and, in the book that follows this one, *OVERRIDING THE EXTINCTION SCENARIO*, *Part Two*, bring in scientific research that can help us further examine

---

[48] I further define and explain this LEAP of mind and focus in other volumes in the series. See *Volume 3*, titled *UNVEILING THE HIDDEN INSTINCT*. See also *Volumes 4 and 5*, titled *HOW TO DIE AND SURVIVE*.

what these books are explaining.[49]

These are profound and unusual ideas. Certainly, take these ideas in as you wish, Reader. For whatever element of communication the **imagination** allows here, consider this all as metaphor, even as fiction or fantasy if you wish, to help consider these ideas.

WIRED-IN
LIMITATIONS

Basically, I am saying that the Human Brain has evolved in such a way as *to limit itself, its definition of itself, and even its own evolution*—therefore to limit and restrict the Earth branch of the Human Species—of the Human Consciousness, to the physical plane.

This limiting wiring of the biological Human Brain is implanted within us, limiting we Earth Humans, and therefore much of Humanity, to less than its full potential even on this physical plane.

Yes, the Human Species is not only a 3-D species. The Human Species is far more, and can assume its rightful place in the cosmos once we Earth Humans free ourselves from limitations imposed upon us.

---

[49] Refer again to the following book, which is *Volume 6* in this *KEYS TO CONSCIOUSNESS AND SURVIVAL SERIES*, titled *OVERRIDING THE EXTINCTION SCENARIO, PART TWO*.

Again note that these are quite possibly limitations imposed upon us via an interfered with, intervened upon, biological evolution—*imposed by intelligent designers and or other powerful trends, forces, and factors.*

SELECTION
FOR WHAT?

Of course, these may also be random, natural, naturally selected, even accidental limitations of natural selection or other evolutionary processes. However, if so, we must still ask the questions:

**"Natural" selection is
selection for what exactly?
And precisely why select these things?**

After all, natural selection suggests that the so-called "fittest" survive, and that therefore the so-called "less fit" characteristics naturally disappear from (or retreat from prevalence or dominance within) the biological gene pool.

However, if our species actually finds its survival in this Earth niche to be threatened, to be in peril, can our species survive?

Let's ask this question this way: If our species finds that it has not "evolved" the characteristics guaranteeing its survival as the Earth niche itself shifts, can our species say that it has selected, evolved, characteristics that may actually

allow it to continue to survive? *Or, might characteristics that allow it to become extinct have been selected?*

Might characteristics that allow us to become extinct been implanted into our design? ARE WE PERHAPS DESIGNED TO DIE? TO DIE OFF? TO ACCEPT THIS AS NORMAL?

SELECTION,
BUT WHY?

Can our species say that it has selected for itself to have a full *rapid adaptability capability, and the means of activating this rapid adaptability capability in order to survive? I describe this capability as:*

**conscious mobility,
conscious meta-adaptation,
along our continuum of consciousness.**

CAN WE META-ADAPT?

Can our species say it has evolved an *extinction proof genetic code*? Why not? Why would we not have evolved this? Are we answering this question based on what we have told ourselves is the purpose (design) of evolution? Are we answering this question based on the limits to knowing that our biological brain provides us?

Are we telling ourselves we cannot have this *extinction proof programming* because we are programmed to believe this is not possible?

Who wrote this script?

How can it be that our species is blocked from fully knowing that it has not only co-evolved with its physical and biological environment, it has also co-evolved with its inter-dimensional environment?

How can it be that our species has not managed to select for, evolve to have, *extinction resistant traits* such as

**rapid interdimensional
awareness,
mobility, and adaptability?**

Is this really a *random* failure of evolution? Or is this some form of success for some higher *species-test extinction-trial* project?

Could it be that our species was indeed limited, locked into an *evolutionary experiment* it could not escape from, much like lab rats in their cages?

DETECTING THE EXTINCTION TRIALS

Let's continue to ask: Are we subjects, unaware unwitting subjects, of what I call…

extinction
trials

… designed to test which (if any) species can or will evolve key adaptive capabilities, key survival characteristics?

**Or, are we perhaps
subjects
in an even larger experiment,
one testing
evolution itself?** …

It is time we dare to consider these questions, questions which have been a long time coming, questions we may be programmed not to think of, not to know to or dare to ask.

OUR SPECIES'
RIGHT TO
EXPANSION

This analysis is about our gaining full understanding of our species' *right to expansion* here and beyond. This is about the essential *liberation* of ourselves, of our species, of Humanity. It is time we set we captives free (captives of the programming, coding, wiring imposed upon us in this physical third dimension evolutionary trek we have been making).

It is time we are free to fully evolve at all levels of our capacity and Humanity, and fully access our *continuum of consciousness, our actual niche.*

ARE COSMOS-RULING INTELLIGENT DESIGNERS
CONDUCTING EXTINCTION TESTS
ON THE SPECIES THEY HAVE DESIGNED?

OUR SPECIES OF
CONSCIOUSNESS:
HUMANITY
→

HUMANITY'S
MOVEMENT
TO ...

...TAKE
REFUGE
IN 3-D

INTERFERENCE
IN CODING → → →
OF BIOLOGICAL
3-D LIFE FORM
FOR EARTH LAB

EARTH LAB
CONDUCTS
SPECIES EXTINCTION
EXPERIMENTS →→→→

EARTH HUMANS BEGIN TO
DETECT THIS EXTINCTION
EXPERIMENT

→→→→→
HUMANITY
SEES THIS
AND REVOLTS

**Figure 15: ARE WE SUBJECTS IN AN
EXTINCTION EXPERIMENT?**

HUMANITY CAN
ASSUME CONTROL OF
ITS OWN EVOLUTION
→→→

151

αΩα

SECTION THREE

**We Are
Not As
Limited As
We May Think**

**Or As We May Have
Been Programmed
To Believe We Are**

Figure 16:
Beyond And Through
Surface Limitations

αΩα

10
THE ARCHAIC
BIOLOGICAL HUMAN BRAIN

Let's look more closely at this biological Human Brain of ours, this brain we are genetically coded to develop as we form in the womb and then through our lives in this physical plane on Earth. This is the brain we carry in our heads. This is the brain we develop within our biological bodies first and foremost via genetic coding, then via interaction between, among, and across: (a) this coding; (b) the neural wiring we are coded to develop; and (c) the environment we live in and co-evolve.

OUR BRAIN IS PROGRAMMED

Certainly, this brain is programmed to do important, essential, things for us such as tell us we are hungry and thus want to eat; tell us we face danger and thus want to fight or run from this danger; tell us we want to engage in sex and thus have a chance of reproducing; tell us we are tired and thus want to sleep; and tell us a range of other things that drive us to engage in primary functions as well as more abstract functions such as problem solving and decision making.

Under directive of genetic coding, our brains form and operate a cellular, neural, and even electronic network of data management (such as perception, intake, processing, storage, and transmission) structures and processes. This brain of ours develops and performs all this *quite obediently*, largely without question. How could our brain do anything else but this, as all this is why this brain exists....

We simply do what our brains tell us to do.
And our brains simply do
what they are coded, programmed, to do.

Certainly, environment influences what our brain does,
however even the way
our brain responds to environmental influence
is managed by
our brain's coding.
Our brain operates us.

This brain of ours is full of neural wiring it is genetically programmed to have and continue to develop. This is biological wiring that forms and directs our biological energy into our brain's various information ...

      -detecting,
      -reading,
      -deciphering,
      -processing,
      -transmission,
      -storage,
      and related tasks.

Our biological brain's bio-wiring is highly vulnerable to programming. In fact, this bio-wiring of our brain exists to: (a) relay to us the *directives of the brain programming* we are coded to carry; and (b) build on additional programming as we have been programmed to do, programming based upon what we describe as experience, learning, feedback, even patterns such as cycles, habits, addictions, and so on.

This is the brain directing us to know what we know and to do what we do. This brain of course also directs the growing, oxygenating, and nourishing of all our biological body systems and their mechanisms.

This includes our brain's directing and developing of: its own nourishing capillaries, with more to particular areas the brain wants to further nourish; its own various and varying degrees of technically adept cell walls with their various selective receptors; its own electrically primed spaces, synapses, between these cell walls; and more. Our Human Brain operates itself as well as its vessel, its vehicle, our Human Body. (Every step of the way, the environment affects the brain's resources, responses, reserves.)

OUR BIOLOGICAL BRAIN
IS CONTROLLING US

All this is clearly there in our brain to allow our brain to engage in its essential perception, data processing, resource, and information management. But look closely, as our powerful, even dictatorial, brain is wired in such a way that

it can and does continuously choose for us:

- what data, information, and signals we do recognize and take in;
- what we do perceive as being there to be perceived;
- how we do read and process what we choose to perceive;
- how we do react or not react to what our brain chooses to read and process;
- how we do continue on with, or change,

    our perceptions and resulting behaviors based on --

    what we believe we choose to perceive and how we choose to react to what we believe we perceive.

All this is determined by our powerful *bio-computer brain*, and the *control functions* of our brain....

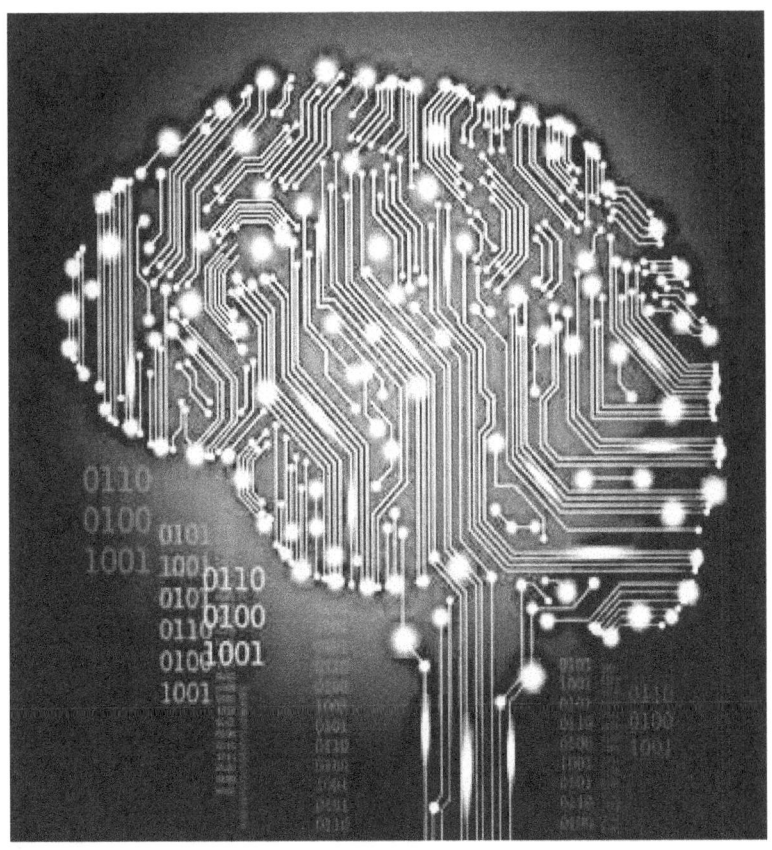

Figure 17:
Coded, Wired, Neural Circuited Brain*

Illustration courtesy of NIAAA/NIDA
*Title of this Figure by Brownemiller,
not this illustration source.

αΩα

11
LIVING UNDER
GENETIC DIRECTIVES

Let's take stock of this complex bio-computer brain we carry around as it operates according to genetic recipe, the programming it wires into itself by genetic directive, and the programming it provides itself for responding to its environment.

Clearly, this organ we call our Human Brain rules us, is there to organize our bodily and mental functions, including our behaviors, thoughts, even our *perceptions of what we believe is reality*, even our interactions with what our brain tells us is our environment.

What profound control our brains have over what we know about who, what, and even where we are, where we actually are. (Of course, we assume this is natural, the way things should be, as we are programmed to do, to assume so.[50])

---

[50] Refer to other books in this *KEYS TO CONSCIOUSNESS AND SURVIVAL SERIES* such as *SEEING BEYOND OUR LINE OF SIGHT*. See also this book in the *FACES OF ADDICTION SERIES*: titled, *SEEING THE HIDDEN FACE OF ADDICTION*. For more information see DrAngela.com.

ABOUT WHERE WE ARE

That we are restricted by our own brain from knowing much more about what and who and where we are is perhaps not surprising, although at the same time, not at all clear to us. The old sayings, "ignorance is bliss" and "what you don't know won't hurt you," are entirely off base here.

It turns out that, when it comes to our survival, what we do not consciously know as a result of our brain blocking our aware consciousness of it, does not necessarily result in bliss. It turns out that, what we don't know may actually hurt us. So, when our brain blocks our awareness of our actual nature and full *options for the focus of our consciousness*, this is or can be dangerous.

We are not consciously fully accessing information that belongs to us, information regarding: (a) our own location in both the physical and the non-physical reality where we actually do concurrently exist; and (b) our own mobility along our own span of being, our own *continuum of consciousness;* and (c) information about what it is that is blocking our access to ourselves, to what we know, to who we are, and to where we are--which is living along and within our own continuum of consciousness.[51]

---

[51] Again, see the book where this *continuum of consciousness* is defined and discussed, *Volume 10* in this series, titled, *SEEING BEYOND OUR LINE OF SIGHT.*

NOTE WE MAY BE BIO-BOTS

Note that while we Human Beings are not robots by most Earth Human engineers' definitions, we are programmed to respond to stimuli both automatically and semi-automatically. Some of our behaviors are automatic on an instinct-driven level (such as our fight or flight reflex), other of our behaviors are readily programmable (such as our stopping at red traffic lights).

We are programmed to do as our brain tells us to do. And our brain is programmed to do as its genetic coding and resulting neural wiring orders and allows us to do. In this way, we are also programmed to be aware of, to know we know, *what our brain is programmed to allow us to be aware of, to think we know we know*. Much of the rest of the information that is in there, deep in our brains, is stored out of our awareness.

Our Human Brain has been coded to develop particular sets of wirings, neural pathways, which are the physical biological form of our programming. As biological robots, we do quite well. We walk and talk and so on....

WE CARRY THE KEY

Seeing the implications of this programming, of this given about our biological selves, is key in this book's discussion of our species' essential next steps in its own evolution.

We have to retrieve the KEY from within our sub- and -un

consciousness to then unlock the door to what is stored there: essential awareness we may need for survival reasons: our actual **location and mobility** along our own continuum of consciousness, the space where we can move ourselves, the focus of our consciousness, as needed.

We must understand our own mobility now to assume our species' birthright, to break free of controls that were either evolved into us by us by "natural" "selection" or by other "natural" "evolutionary" factors, or were perhaps implanted into our brain's wiring and its coding by accident—

> **or again perhaps,**
> **by some external influence,**
> **factor, force, or intelligence.**

However we have arrived at this point, daily we know more about this bio-technical marvel, our Human Brain. We see how "automatic" (or at least not discretionary from an awareness standpoint) the majority of our functions and perceptions are. As programmed and programmable beings, we are in a sense bio-bots, aren't we?

Question: if we are bio-bots, biological robots, whose robots are we? Are we simply a random development of nature? Or is something more intentional going on here?

Once we wonder such things, it is ever more important to take a close look at this thing, this biological brain, that apparently controls us—

or that perhaps even allows
something other than itself to control us.

Does our brain serve as the main frame or perhaps the physical conduit for an *externally originated control function, an externally driven executive control source? Can we ever know the answer this such questions?*

Are we allowed to know?
Are we allowed to
be able to know?

ARE WE
ALLOWED TO HAVE
FULL DATA INTAKE CAPACITY?

Our brains have stored within them the *capacity to direct* our senses to constantly take in and perceive *selected* "information."

We know consciously *only some* of what all our brains direct our senses to perceive and then direct our brain to process, some of this for use by our conscious awareness. As for the rest of what we are perceiving, or on some level choosing to allow ourselves to perceive, and then processing, we may also know about some of this on our sub- and un- conscious levels.

How much of our sub- and un- conscious levels can we

access? How much of what goes on in our brain and its mind "out of our own awareness" can we actually bring into our own awareness?

On an ongoing basis, we are presented with, often even receiving, data, information, we do not "consciously" know we are receiving. Our biological brains are *filtering, even determining, what we perceive of our reality for us*. (See the depiction of this filtering in Figures 18 and 19.)

And, we are even sub- and un- consciously choosing to ignore certain data, to *not know* certain things, while not consciously knowing we are making such a choice. *So much of what our controlling brains are doing is being done out of our conscious awareness.*

SO MUCH OF
WHAT WE DO NOT KNOW

So much of *what we do not know we know* is blocked from our awareness by our own brain, ostensibly to protect us from information overload. Indeed, as a result of evolution or some other factor, we Humans are easily over stimulated, overloaded, burdened by too much of everything, even at times by too many choices.

We have therefore developed a blocking, or screening, or filtering process (or all three of these) to protect us from what is commonly described as TMI--too much information. This process has been developed rather than develop an effective

cataloging and accessing function allowing us locate and access to what all is stored within us.

Our brain is designed to *filter out* the seeming "noise," to help us survive being barraged by incoming data, to avoid breaking with data overload. This *filtering out* makes sense, yes.

And of what our brain does let into our awareness, our brain organizes, prioritizes, categorizes, interprets, performs mental and even emotional operations on, and then tells us what to do with and about these "perceptions" and this "information." *What our brain decides we do not need to know is filtered out of our awareness.*

**But what else might be
being filtered out?
And why?**

CONTROLLING
EXECUTIVE LEVEL
BRAIN FUNCTION

What the AWARE Conscious Self thinks it is, thinks it perceives, thinks it knows, and any information this Aware Conscious Self has to work with, is largely determined by the controlling executive-level of the Biological Brain. This brain is performing this executive level information processing and *filtering process* in its generating and *controlling of us* — of our Un-, Sub-, and Aware Conscious Selves (who of course are not always working in unison or even conjointly).

This Executive Brain does all this according to its genetic coding and the neural wring it is coded to develop and implement. The capacity of the Aware Conscious Self to consciously intake information, and what information it does intake, process, and then bring to its own attention, is determined by the Executive Brain and the programming inherited by and directing the Executive Brain. This is the basis of the biologically based Conscious Self (which is not the entire Conscious Self who our biological brain is allowing us only minimal access to).

EXECUTIVE CONTROL
OF CONSCIOUS SELF?

The brain's executive control function (the ECF) operates primarily under the radar, below the level of our conscious awareness, thus independently of us, of the aware us. However, our brain's executive control function does not operate independently of our biology.

Where we are perhaps able to be free is in the realm of our non-physical selves. This is *what* of *who* we are, that is not, or not need not be, biologically based.

Whether or not we do have a consciousness that can exist independently of biology, I suggest we can develop or evolve this. This is the SELF that can best survive along the continuum of consciousness. It is essential we see this now.

A *Conscious Self* that could be independent, not in any way tied to or surviving because of biology, is at least somewhat conceivable. If this independent, free-standing, Conscious Self could exist, it would not be ruled by this biologically based controlling Executive Biological Brain. Even while living in biological bodies, we would have direct unmediated access to our actual selves, to our own continuum of consciousness.

Where we required expert information management, cataloging, and processing, we would consciously be determining what may and may not be appropriately taking place out of our awareness. *Our ECF would report to us, not we to it. We would be its master. After all, this is our own brain we are talking about, yes?*

WE CAN ALLOW OURSELVES TO ASK

We can ask: What part of what our brain tells us is our reality actually exists? What part of what we believe is our reality is what the Executive Control Function operating our biological brain tells us is the reality we are allowed to "know," or at least to believe we are living within?

And, if this executive (control function) that controls us lets us know only some of our reality, how much more of our reality is this executive blocking out of our awareness?

SO ... HOW CAN WE KNOW

How then can we monitor what our brains are not telling us? How then can we consciously know whether we are missing out on important, even essential, information relevant to our survival?

Given that our biological Human Brain is an old model, one that may not be keeping up with the survival pressures we are now facing, how can we be sure that even the sub- and un- conscious levels of this brain are prepared to deal with current and future shifts in our niche, in our environment?

We cannot, fully aware, "consciously," access in full what is not moving into our *biological-brain-generated sense of our awareness. The wall is up, the curtain is closed.* We cannot monitor what all we may actually know, what all we may be perceiving.

**We are
designed
not to know (or be aware of)
all that we know.**

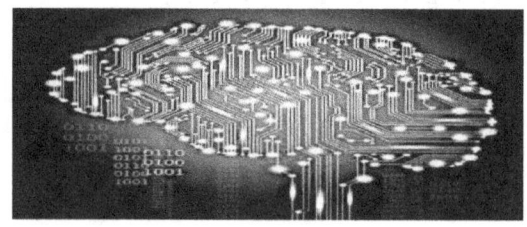

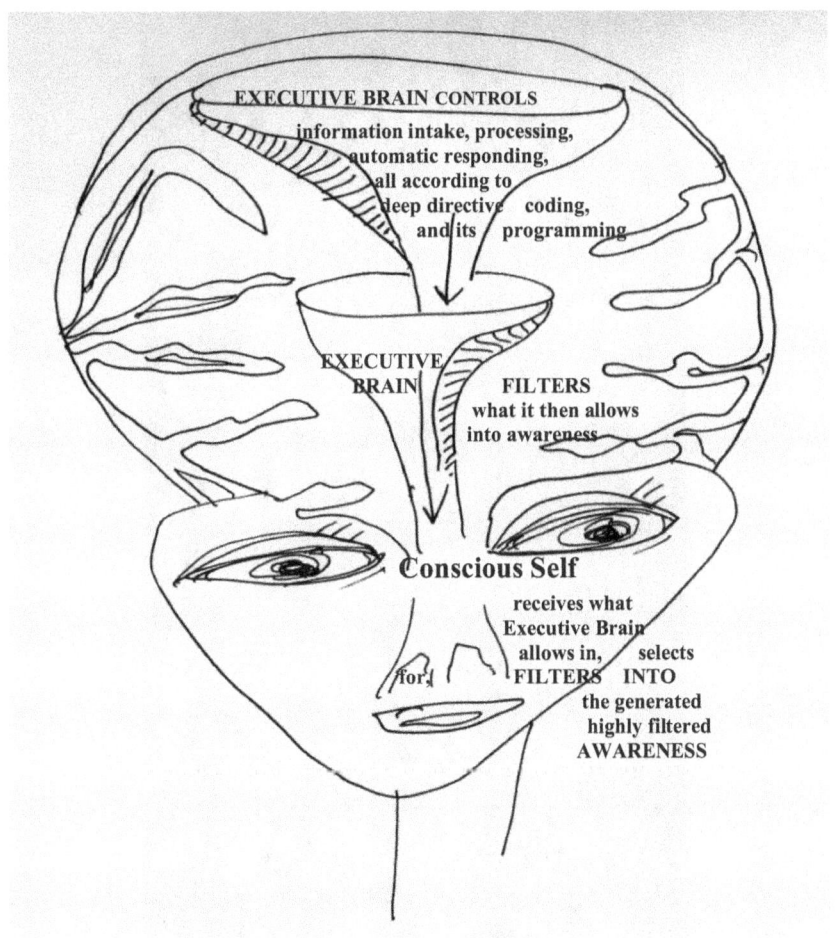

Figure 18:
Human Brain's Executive Filtering Function

(1) EXECUTIVE BRAIN CONTROLS information intake, processing, automatic responding, all according to deep directive coding and its programming.

(2) EXECUTIVE BRAIN FILTERS AND SELECTS all of what it then allows into our seeming awareness.

(3) CONSCIOUS SELF receives what Executive Brain allows in, selects for, FILTERS INTO, our generated and highly filtered awareness.

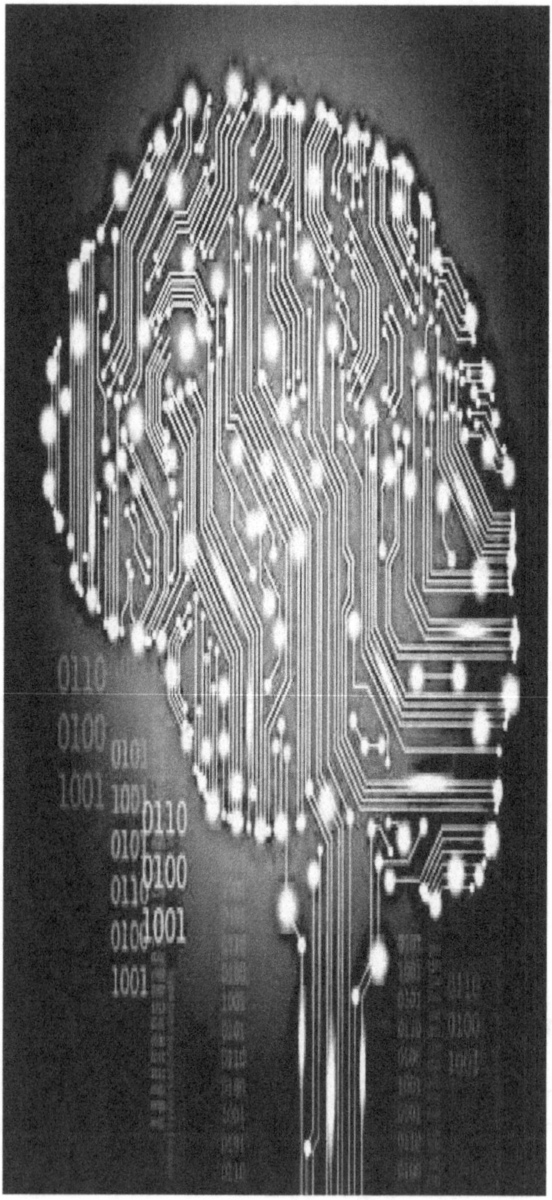

Again we see that...

Our brains are deciding for us what we can know and what we can consciously know we know.

At the same time, our brains are deciding for us what we cannot know and cannot know we do not know.

What if there is key information about us and our capabilities, even about our consciousness-es, buried deep inside us-- being locked away out of our awareness by the blocking, suppressing, dominating done by our perhaps antiquated genetic coding, or by something else?

Call this an accident of evolution, or call this situation the product of some intervention or experiment. Whatever has brought us here, it is time for us to look at our situation and gain some form of *conscious involvement* in our next steps.

Our brains block us from being consciously aware of many of the choices our brains are making. Some of these choices are **to *not* see, to *not* take in, information**—even what may be essential information. Other of these choices are to process this information but not to bring all aspects of this processed information to our conscious awareness.

Our brains are thus so very selective in what they allow us to know, and in what they allow us to know we know. **Our brains limit what of ourselves we can access.**

THIS IS NOT ABOUT OVERLOAD

Sure, we tell ourselves our brains are keeping us from overload. However, who is to say what our conscious brains can actually handle? Who is to say whether and why our conscious brains have or have not been allowed (or allowed to evolve) the capacity they need to fully aware and consciously know, access, all they need to know? Couldn't effective means of access have been evolved, rather than lock us out of full access to ourselves for the sake of seeming efficiency?

The capacity is likely there; we walk around with brains that may have far greater capacity for awareness than we currently consciously access. Again…

the primary matter is
our programming
not to have conscious access
to our own brain's
own awareness capacity.

We must consider the real possibility that:

There may be, within our biological brains, a range of (accidentally arrived at, or naturally evolved, or purposefully implanted) *blocks to full awareness capacity*, a range of blocks to full data recognition, intake, and processing, and stops to alternate data selection. Our brains may be programmed to only perceive what they are allowed to perceive by our coding, our programming.

Yes, our brains may be programmed to allow us to know only certain things, certain things that *support the reality* our brains are programmed to define for us, to commit us to. Are our biological brains constructing our reality for us?

Our brains hold a great deal in our un-conscious, hold it back from our aware consciousness. Certainly, this function can protect us from deeply buried trauma and other injuries to our minds and psyches. However, this function itself is likely outdated and not serving us efficiently, or correctly for that matter.

So we know only some of what our senses actually sense. At least consciously we know only some. *But how much more do we know than we realize we know?*

And can we access that deeper level information while fully conscious and alert?

Are there awareness-es we can directly access outside of what our biological brain permits? Can we know things without moving information within and among pre-set brain cell and synapse pathways?

(NOTE: Certainly, there are methods such as hypnosis, EMDR, some psychoactive treatments, and other therapies, that tell patients and clients that these methods reach into buried "stuff" within their minds. While there is great debate regarding the risks and responsibilities of working to dig into the mind-brain behind what appears to be the conscious self, these approaches can be useful when conducted with great care, and by highly trained and certified practitioners who have years of training before conducting these methods. Do note that these approaches do not reach into the level this book is discussing, the level far beneath our selves, beneath the selves our brains tell us we have and are. This is another level of this work, a level we cannot reach by working through the biological brain per se.)

Imagine
what the removal of
the biological filter controlling our
thoughts, perceptions, awareness-es,
might bring us.

(NOTE AGAIN: While some gurus, some self-help guides, some religious teachers, even various proponents of psychoactive drugs and medicines, may tell us they have the way to access what I am talking about here, they are not entirely on topic, not this topic of this book. They are still bound by the processes being directed by our biological

brains. They are still bound by the presumed ties of our consciousness to our biology, as all their methods access us through our biological bodies and brains.)

DO WE KNOW WHAT
OUR BRAIN IS DOING FOR (TO) US?

How much can we access, consciously know, of what our brains are picking up sub- and even un- consciously, of what information there is for us within ourselves and out there, on other levels and in other dimensions of our reality?

Do we actually have far more **interdimensional awareness and reality** than our brain allows us to be consciously aware of?

How much of **our own expansive continuum of consciousness** is our brain allowing us to be aware of, and to access? What about this continuum we do live along and within is our brain allowing us to see?

Why have we been evolved or designed not to have the option, in any given moment, to fully access the information and knowledge we already carry within us?

Yes, we can grasp bits and pieces of this information. However, **we are wired not to fully access it**. We have been led (by our brains) to understand that consciously being aware of as much as our brains know would be impossible, or at least overwhelming for us. Our brains are thus wired not to be able to do this, not to be able to allow everything within

our brains into our consciousness-es, not to be able to do this for (what our brains are coded to tell us is) efficiency's sake.

What
obedient beings
we are.

As I discuss further in the coming chapters of this and the following book, we Humans have stored within our biological brains, have had genetically coded and programmed into our brains:

**the capacity to
automatically block
from our aware conscious level
the information
we apparently do not "need" to know
on this so-called conscious basis.**

Something in our coding, our programming, is telling us that what we do not know, we do not have to know. This is a limitation we did not ask for, one that was somehow placed within us. *See my discussion of controlling and reality dictating brain functions such as attentional bias, in the following book (OVERRIDING THE EXTINCTION SCENARIO, PART TWO) and in other books in this series.*[52]

---

[52] See also next sections of this (and also the following) OVERRIDING THE EXTINCTION SCENARIO book, as well as other books on reading list at end of this present book, such as, *SEEING THE HIDDEN FACE OF*

Oddly however, there is a great deal of "stuff" or "noise" we consciously know that has very little use, even little if any entertainment use, and likely little if any survival value. So, some *UN*essential information seeps into our aware consciousness while some (or much) of what may be highly essential does not. How can we know?

**Is this a
filtering malfunction of our brain
or a programmed-in control of us?**

**Could this be a
fatal flaw
designed into us,
into our programming,
into our brain's design?**

Are we designed to distract ourselves, to clutter our consciousness-es with trivia so as to miss out on truth? Are we designed to fail? Is this design driving an implanted extinction scenario we do not see for what it is, one we are wired not to see playing out? Are we programmed to live in an eyes-wide-shut level of understanding?

Seriously, we must ask whether natural selection actually

ADDICTION, as well as the *INTERNATIONAL COLLECTION ON ADDICTIONS, Volume Two, Psychobiological Profiles*.

would select for, evolve into us, this sort of not knowing[53] (and this sort of not knowing what it is we do not know) as a survival of the fittest mechanism.

Does this mean that, the less we know about what we actually do know, the less we know about our actual continuum of consciousness, the more "fit" we are, the more "selected for" we are? This sounds wrong, ludicrous, absurd, more like a story someone has told us to keep us ignorant and controllable.

How readily a population, even an entire species, can be controlled by keeping that population, that species, uninformed, unaware, not knowing, not accessing what it knows.

Would natural selection evolve into us a brain that can block us from fully knowing and fully deciding for ourselves what we need to know on an aware conscious basis? I say no, unless this has been a highly flawed natural selection process--or something else, some other process or intervention, or experiment perhaps.

IT IS TIME

It is time now for us to interrogate this limit setting and

---

[53] I discuss the neuroscience of this process in sections of the following book and in other books, see reading list at end of this present book.

filtering our brains do, this control of what we know, and of what we know we know, and of what we know we know we know…and maybe even, of what we are not allowed to know.

Of course, we are finding that, to at least some extent, we do have some capacity to train ourselves to pull otherwise sub- and unconscious awareness-es into our consciousness-es. Sometimes this is a rather simple expanding of awareness.

For example, one who stares at a field full of faces in a room full of strangers, or at a hill full of wildflowers on a hill full of wild vegetation, sees only the crowd or the field. But once the names of the specific strangers in the room or of the specific types of plants on the hill are known, then one sees a room with specific people in it and a hill full of specific wildflowers. We see that identifying specific information allows us to recognize it, and then to take this information in.

I have found *information identification* essential in teaching and in clinical work. I believe that this *information identification* can, on another level, serve to bring our species access to what it needs to know about itself to survive the coming shifts and challenges.

We can train our minds to identify information our brains are blocking us from accessing. While a range of valuable suggestions exist for so doing, these suggestions are not addressing the larger issue this and other books in this series are centered on:

WE ARE AN INTERDIMENSIONAL LIFE FORM whose biological brain cannot fully access and does not fully allow us to know: our actual SELVES, our personal consciousnesses, who exist along our own *continuum of consciousness,* who can be acccessed even independent of our biology.

**What our brain is
not allowing us to know
must be identified
and reached beyond.**

Once we understand what this process is, then this is a meta-perceptual and a meta-cognitive shift we can consciously make. I call this *the conscious information, and interdimensional existence, identification process.*

And, at about this moment in my workshops, I am again told by some audience members that there are various researchers, spiritualists, and others who can tell us of other routes to knowing, such as religious, meditative, psychological, emotional, psychoactive drug, and other processes.

And I respond that some *but not all* of these processes (now so popular) can be useful and even offer insights. However, I go on to add that:

- Once a process does involve an *externally determined*

philosophical or biochemical format, it also *dictates* to us, and to our brain, what and how we, and our brains, will perceive and receive. Moreover, the biological brain remains the conduit, the mediator, of the processing even when provided these external aids.

- So, going to these external processes to shift and take control of a *pattern of perception and knowing **we want to reach independent of our biology**,* is sharing the biological brain's control with other controlling factors *rather than taking ourselves back to our actual SELVES, reaching deeply into ourselves to contact who we actually are, our own personal aware consciousness who can exist even independent of biology.*

- We must access and address the control of us by our brain's programming to <u>*limit what we know about ourselves as being a species of consciousness living along our own continuum of consciousness. Ultimately, where we actually are is who we actually are, and yet this is not part of our brain's work to bring this into our conscious awareness.*</u> <u>***We already exist within and as the terrain of, our own consciousness, our own continuum of consciousness.***</u> <u>*(This is indeed the PATTERN TERRAIN defined in other books in this series, such as SEEING BEYOND OUR LINE OF SIGHT and NAVIGATING LIFE'S STUFF, BOOK TWO.)*</u>

- Yes, many will argue that their beliefs, practices, and or drugs will indeed give people access to what they

term, "higher consciousness." However, this again is not direct access, not guaranteed access to one's own un-interfered with consciousness. Of course, some form of alternate consciousness may be reached or appear to be reached by beliefs and practices and even medicines and drugs, however has it sprung directly from the Human Consciousness unaided, unguided, unfiltered by biological controls?

No. All roads do not lead to the same place. And beware of the street signs directing us to some place these mislabeled street signs are defining for us....

I am not critiquing these external processes designed to shift what I call *awareness control*. What I am saying here is that ultimately what is most ideal is that we can take conscious control of our own awareness without drugs or philosophies or particular practices being processed by our biological brains and bodies, and marketed to us by biological brains and bodies, as awareness and or heightened awareness.

Reader, ultimately,
the key to you is you.
**If you do not have the key to you,
if this key has been withheld
or taken from you,
then take this key back.**

AND, AS YOU TAKE YOUR KEY BACK,

ALWAYS STAY WITH YOURSELF:
KEEP YOUR OWN COUNSEL.[54]

Too often, what looks like you to you
may be some
idea or chemical or practice telling you it is you
when it is not you.

If you look closely, dare to look closely,
you will see who you are,
sense the path to yourself,
be able to directly access you for you.

YOU CAN DIS-INTERMEDIATE
(remove the executive, the middle man from)
YOUR AWARENESS,
YOUR EXPERIENCE,
OF EXISTING.

YOU CAN MAKE
DIRECT CONTACT
WITH YOUR BRAIN, MIND, CONSCIOUSNESS.

YOU CAN
DISINTERMEDIATE
YOUR ACCESS TO
YOUR OWN AWARENESS,
TO YOUR OWN CONSCIOUSNESS,
TO YOUR SELF.

---

[54] See more regarding this taking of our KEYS back in the *KEYS TO SELF®
Program* material at DrAngela.com.

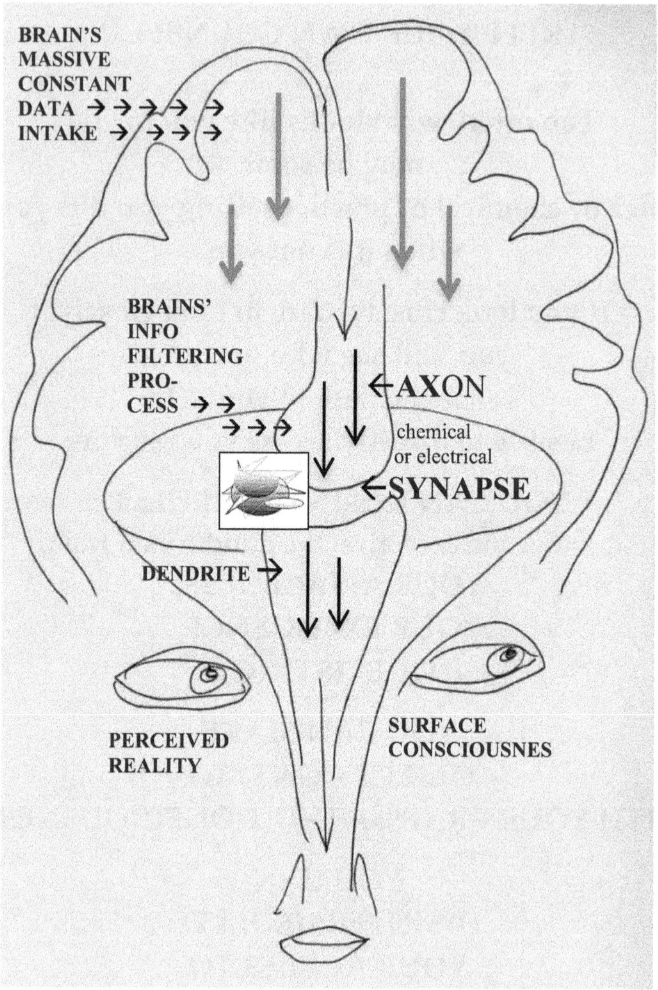

BRAIN'S MASSIVE CONSTANT DATA → → → → → INTAKE → → → →

BRAINS' INFO FILTERING PRO- CESS → → → → →

←AXON

chemical or electrical

←SYNAPSE

DENDRITE →

PERCEIVED REALITY

SURFACE CONSCIOUSNES

Figure 19:
Brain's Synaptic Control As Filtering Process

= *what of who we are and of what we can know we may or may not have access to*

αΩα

12
MEET OUR BRAIN'S POWERFULLY CONTROLLING EXECUTIVE CONTROL FUNCTION

Most organizations develop a hierarchy to operate themselves and their members. It *appears* that the Human Brain does this as well.[55]

I emphasize that it *appears* this is so, as, even in the face of marked and significant scientific study, we cannot specify for certain, on a one to one, electrical impulse to electrical impulse, basis, *all that actually operates* all the micro-level workings of the Human Brain, let alone its most elusive aspects.

We can track (via brain scan, etc.) oxygen, glucose, other nutrients, even electrical impulses, all moving through the brain. And while we can associate some of this tracking with various mental activities, we cannot absolutely entirely, directly and precisely, on a one to one point to point basis,

---

[55] Of course, we can only know, only be aware of, what our brain allows us to believe we know and are aware of. So what we know, even about our brain's hierarchies of **thought management and thought control**, is generally what our brain allows us to know. See other books and presentations by this author on thought control, as per reading list at the end of this present book.

already associate any of this with the minute workings of thought organization itself, or for that matter with what we call *our consciousness*.

BEHIND
THE CURTAIN

Among the presently defined functions of the Human Brain, the function most likely to dominate us, largely from behind what I call the *curtain of conscious awareness*, is what some scientists indeed do describe as the "executive control function."

This function is not something we operate fully consciously. Indeed, as noted in earlier chapters of this book, this executive control function (ECF) is *working behind the scenes* much of the time.

We may bring bits of this function into our awareness (in daily problem solving, for example). However, when we do so, we are only contacting the tip of the iceberg, if that.

**Much of what
our executive control function
is doing is
controlling our awareness of
its presence itself.**

We believe we are, and indeed are, conscious of a great amount. However, comparatively, this is a minor amount we

are allowed to consciously access, a minor amount that we **think** *we are conscious of, that our brain allows us to be conscious of.*[56])

It is important to see that this executive control function is *central in our relationship to our own brains (or to* **what we think is our own brain-mind**), as well as to the more obvious functional aspects of our brain. Science is continuing to add to and even revise its descriptions of this function; however, there are already some basics to know or at least to ask about executive control.

WHO HIRED
THIS EXECUTIVE
TO RUN YOU?

As the **executive control function** is just that, the executive that controls your brain's so-called "higher" functions, it is a good idea to think about who or what this executive is....

---

[56] Again, I note that although terms/phrases such as "what we are *conscious of*" and "being *conscious of*" are popular jargon and commonly used, these overlap with discussions of our consciousness and of what is frequently called our "higher" consciousness. Hence, to distinguish the line of inquiry shared in this book, I use the phrase <u>*aware* **consciousness**</u> when I am referring to what we are actually aware of (or at least think we are aware of), allowing for the large body of our consciousness we also carry or have some access to yet are not aware of. As I explain earlier in this book, I view our awareness as the ***operant arm*** of our consciousness, as being, when alerted, our rightful access to our actual consciousness.

Now, be aware that *you cannot even think about this executive without this executive knowing you are doing so.*

So, you have no privacy as you ask about this exec, this executive control function controlling your thoughts, about who it is and why it is here.

You have no privacy when you wonder whether this exec can allow you any thought control detection power of your own without this exec being in command.

You cannot ask questions about this exec without this exec knowing you are asking. This exec is even in control of how much you can consciously engage in, be aware of.

WHERE DOES THIS EXECUTIVE LIVE?

Our brain's **thought-controlling and organizing** executive control function involves the frontal lobe, among other parts of the brain. The frontal lobe is the most recent area of the brain to "appear" in mammalian evolution here on Earth, and contains the precious prefrontal cortex where the complex cognitive behavior, decision making, behavior modification, personality expression, and other so-called "more complex and advanced" functions arise.

Basically, what Humans consider their "advanced" thinking is prefrontal cortex (PFC) work. It is the precious PFC that carries out the executive function which engages in complex

processes such as differentiating between conflicting thoughts, differentiating (and thus defining on a very deep level) what is or may be a "good or a bad idea," goal identification and realization, perception of outcomes, and other processes.

In addition to the PFC, the executive control function (ECF) actually also involves the brain's basal ganglia (at the base of our forebrain area) and brain's thalamus (located between the cerebral cortex, the outer layer of the brain consisting of folded gray matter which is believed to play a central role in consciousness, and the midbrain located of course in the mid brain area and addressing slightly "lower" functions such as vision, hearing, motor control, sleep-wake alertness, temperature control).

However, it appears that the frontal lobe's PFC is the part of the brain that engages in, largely controls, the *actual higher order processing involving various higher levels of abstraction* that our scientists tell us appeared "late" in our evolution. Interestingly, the executive control function itself is said to have evolved still more recently, as it emerged primarily once the PFC evolved.

It is said that, as we "progressed" on through our evolution, as we began to think for "ourselves," to really think (in terms of what appears to be uniquely Human higher order abstraction), the executive CONTROL function (ECF) came in to "help" us, or I say, to *regulate and control us*.

Yes, we can say we naturally evolved, selected for, this ECF

(exec function) to help ourselves. And perhaps we did evolve this executive control naturally, by random event or accident of nature.

What a powerful evolutionary event, one that has empowered our brains and the biologically based minds they generate.

IF WE HAD HAD A SAY

However, we must ask ourselves: If we had had a say in our own evolution, would we consciously have chosen to have a function we could not consciously control, one we could not always be consciously aware of, *telling us how and what to think*?

Surrendering conscious control risks succumbing to programming and or to outside or invisible control.

This means we do not know what is organizing or even conducting (managing) a significant portion of our thinking.

Again referring to natural selection, we can allow ourselves to ask:

> *Did the so-called survival of the so-called fittest require the* **surrendering by** *our increasingly complex and extensive brain* **of control over its own** *increasingly more complex and extensive thinking?*

Did we evolve, even select for, the invisible *thought control* we are today experiencing at the "hands" of our brain's executive control function?

Can it be true that survival of the fittest selected for (evolved) our brain's executive control function? Can it be true that we naturally evolved into ourselves this function operating within us and upon us, controlling our thinking, from _behind the curtain of our awareness? Really?_

Or, might we, for a moment, consider the possibility that perhaps, just maybe, this *thought control* was <u>implanted</u> into our genetic coding, thereby into our brain's wiring? Does the design of our biological brain carry and implement the powerful directive this design received to control us as biological beings?

Could there have been an intelligent designer who implanted executive control to set a ceiling on us, on our awareness, on own mental activity, even on our evolution into our own rightful territories of consciousness where we already do live, even on our access to our own continuum of consciousness?[57]

**What a convenient way to control a captive:
just place the lock, the boundary, within.**

---

[57] Again, refer to *Volume 10* in this series, *SEEING BEYOND OUR LINE OF SIGHT*, and *Volume 3* in this series, *UNVEILING THE HIDDEN INSTINCT.*

I say that this powerful and valuable, even essential, executive control function *is* indeed also **thought control,** that we have to see that this *is* thought control. Something we do not have *aware conscious access to* is controlling our thinking. Pretty *un*intelligent design if you ask me, a questionable step in evolution … unless this is indeed something a higher intelligence intelligently, purposefully, implanted into a captive species, into us, perhaps for species control, and or for experimental mind or awareness control purposes… **perhaps, to block us from full access to ourselves.**

Of course, it is likely that this powerful ECF did evolve as a positive step in our evolution. We have reached great heights as a result of the brain power this ECF has given us.

Yet, with this brain power the ECF has given us, there is also a restriction on our accessing what is there in our brain behind this executive who is clearly in charge. Could there have been another development, one secretly drawing away from us and utilizing this great power we have been given, while forming a means of blocking our conscious access to all this power within us?

Whose story is this? Whose ECF is this?

Maybe evolution did generate this all commanding ECF. Or, maybe something else did. Perhaps we are indeed lab rats in some kind of **extinction trial** where species are studied for their survival capabilities (Adaptability? Ingenuity? Awareness?) when under shifting environmental pressures.

ELEMENTS OF
EXECUTIVE THOUGHT CONTROL

This executive thought control falls into at least three areas: thought organization, thought regulation, and thought hierarchy.

The mind's executive work apparently includes but is not limited to mental processes such as these I list here *(with my comments regarding each function in italics)*:

- identifying, even dictating to us,
  what is "relevant" information ...
  (and leaving out information it deems is not relevant for us to consciously know);

- remembering and utilizing instructions ...
  (the instructions we should be following according to this executive);

- planning and prioritizing ...
  (as this exec wants us to);

- selecting tasks to be attended to ...
  (the tasks this exec wants us to attend to);

- monitoring and then selecting
  which stimuli to be conscious of ...
  (and which to not know are out there);

- self control ...
  (*or the exec's control of us making it look and feel like self control*);

- decision making ...
  (*making decisions the exec wants us to make*);

- moral reasoning ...
  (*according to morals we construct based on orders of this executive in control*).

WITHOUT OUR CONSCIOUS CONTROL

Nothing here says that this ECF is not essential. Our brain's executive control function reviews and organizes what our brain thinks, makes it possible for us to manage a great deal of information and responses to information, and manages complexity for us, at least whenever this thinking is somewhat complex.

Yet, as this ECF moved into us, developed or evolved into our brains, particular control mechanisms emerged. I note again here that this executive control function is something controlling us *without our having full conscious control of it*.

And actually, this function organizes all that our brain *thinks*

it thinks, and in fact only allows us *aware conscious access* to what it deems right for us to have aware conscious access to.

We are not given
aware conscious access to
most of the control over us.

After all, this mysterious executive sitting there within our brains, this commanding function, thinks many things we are not aware it is thinking, chooses for us many things we are not aware it is choosing, decides for us many things we are not aware it is deciding.

This function works within us largely on a sub- or un-conscious level to process, prioritize, organize, analyze data and information. Executive control indeed does control the perception, intake, classification, prioritization, use of, and response to, incoming information to such a degree that:

we cannot know
what we know
without this function allowing us
to know we know.

POWERFUL OPERATION

We have this powerful control operation, this executive, running us at all times. Yet, we are largely unaware of its existence, let alone its workings.

We are programmed not to hold in our conscious awareness most all the management activities our brain's ECF is engaged in. For the most part, our executive control function's ubiquitous presence is something we are not paying attention to, are not aware of, and know only a fraction about. What we see or sense of this ECF is merely the tip of the iceberg.

Our not knowing much, and not thinking much, about our brain's executive control function is not surprising. Our lives, friends, and activities do not point to this function despite the fact this function is working at all times.

How many people call you on any given day and ask to speak to your executive control function? (They might ask for you, or your spouse, or your mother, your father, your children, your boss, someone else. However, they do not ask for your executive control function.)

How many times a day do you ask your brain to allow you to communicate directly with your brain's executive control function? (Try doing this more often and see what you find. In other books, I detail exercises such as this. See the reading list at the end of this present book.)

Of course, studying or even cramming for an exam may move a person in the direction of bringing a vague awareness of the brain's executive control function into some degree of aware conscious contact, may bring a person to tell his or her brain

to remember this, learn that, know how to apply this formula.

However, much of the time, even when we tell ourselves to do such things, we are not actually confronting our executive control function (ECF) fully consciously, and then consciously putting this ECF to work for us.

And we are not taking the control of our brains and minds away from the hidden executive running us, this entity we did not consciously hire for the job. **(Evolution or something else hired this ECF to do this for and to us.)**

We are not telling this executive, this gatekeeper on our access to ourselves, to our brains, to our minds, that we wish to be in control of this gate. We are not saying that we wish to have this controlling executive consciously report to <u>us</u>, <u>to our awareness</u>. We are not saying stop, change things, reverse the power structure here, as we do not want to continue under your complete control. **Yet, it is time to say this.**

This ECF gatekeeper is *even controlling our access to our own continuum of consciousness, to our own territory, to what may be our own <u>survival territory</u>*. We must wonder why.[58]

However, be careful here, as we cannot simply fire this invasive controlling executive. We need the commanding presence and service of this ECF in complex areas such as decision making, planning, and making judgements. Without

---

[58] See the *EARTH URGENT TRILOGY* books for details on the matter of SURVIVAL TERRITORY.

a substitute organizer and thinker, without ourselves becoming *highly conscious captains of ourselves*, we may risk slipping into mental blither. As biological Humans living in 3-D reality, we need our brain's executive control function. However, we need to know what it may be masking.

OUR AWARENESS
IS VAGUE
OR SHUT OUT

Again, our awareness of our executive control function is vague where this awareness exists at all. Moreover, even our *awareness of our awareness is rather elusive.* There are moments we feel aware of something, moments we tell ourselves we are aware. However, what is this awareness we are referring to?

How aware is this awareness we think we have when we think we have it? What exactly is this awareness and exactly how do we know this?

Of course, as noted earlier in this book, we are led to believe (by our brain) that we would be too overloaded to function were we to consciously know everything. Therefore, as this belief tells us, we (our brain) shuts out information (our brain tells us) we do not "need" to know. (See the following book, *OVERRIDING THE EXTINCTION SCENARIO, PART TWO,* for more on this programmed-in *overload control function,* as well as the programmed-in *overload illusion*).

We do this rather than knowing how to directly access and control/manage the full range of our own brains, the massive amount of brain we carry around within us without being consciously aware of using while using (or while it is being used).

Similar to the way we shut out conscious awareness of "too much" incoming information to avoid "information overload," we also shut out *conscious awareness* of much of our brain's very own executive control function. We do this, at least ostensibly we do this, because we are told by our brain that we cannot handle knowing this much, not consciously. The mental desktop, the brain space, our brain has evolved for us is too limited to hold that much data in the aware conscious realm. So, the brain's shutting material out of our awareness is almost a given.

Really? So we have chosen to evolve this shutting out? Likely not, as we were not engaged in *conscious evolution (or conscious design) of ourselves and our brains, of our consciousness-es themselves.* So who or what evolved this limited conscious brain space, and the related shutting out, into our brain function?

**Do we really
want to believe that
our evolution selected for us, for our brains, to
shut out what we may need to know to survive?**

Did we really evolve this not-knowing

as a survival function?

Do we really believe we cannot find ways to have our magnificent brains organize incoming information so that we can consciously access and sort through all of it on an as needed basis, to see what our conscious minds may be missing and blocking out, to see what we may need to know to be safe, and well, and to thrive? To survive?

Or is this what we have been led to believe, programmed to feel is the case, that we are this limited? That we need to be this limited to function, to live?

WE DO KNOW WE ARE BEINGS

We Humans know we are beings. We seem to know we are beings with brains. We seem to even realize we have some degree of conscious awareness of ourselves. Yet, we seem to miss out on some of the ongoing front and center activities of our own brains, activities going on every single moment we are living in these physical bodies.

As beings with brains, we for the most part feel, if we feel anything at all about this, that we are not able to watch consciously our brain's executive control mechanisms at work. Sure, these mechanisms are designed (or evolved, or perhaps implanted into our genetic coding) to be sub- and unconscious level functions, to operate under our awareness, under our aware conscious radar.

This apparently is a good thing, or so we assume, or so we are led to believe, or so we tell ourselves and are told by our brain and its executive control function. After all, without our ECF we might be nowhere near where we are today, in terms of our mental functioning.

Whatever is the "right" answer to this matter of why and whether we need more conscious access to our brain's executive control function, we can see this primary issue:

**There are things going on in our brains
that we are not consciously aware of.**

**We have been evolved
not to be able to be fully consciously aware.
Thus, there are things going on in our brains
that we do not consciously
"know" are going on there.**

**Once we realize this,
do we want to ask
whether there is a way
we can be fully conscious of
what is going on in our own heads?**

**Yes, we do want to know
whether there might have been a way
for our brain to be designed
to allow this access to and efficient cataloging of
all stored in there behind the curtain.**

αΩα

13
WHO OR WHAT
HAS CONTROL
OVER OUR
COMPLEX BRAIN
AND DOES THIS MATTER?

Alright, yes, our brain is so incredibly complex, with so many billions if not trillions of ongoing micro-actions and transactions taking place, that we say we cannot consciously know all this at once. We ask, who wants to have this much information overload at any time let alone all the time?

And we do think of this as overload. Our brain is programmed, coded, wired, to tell us that this much data/information is information/data overload.

But here again is the bigger question....

Why do we have brains that were not evolved or designed to have full access capacity, that were not designed to *consciously* manage as much information as they take in and process?

Why do we have these fantastic bio-computers in our heads?

Why have we built into these buried bio-computers these *limits* on our ability to access all they (we) know, even when more of the data in these bio-computers is needed? Did we develop or design this limit of ourselves for ourselves?

ARE THERE BUILT IN BLOCKS
TO KNOWING SOME THINGS?

Could there be a purpose in our
not having the capacity to consciously access
the secrets we carry within our own heads?

This issue here is about the
limits on our ability to know ...
what these
bio-computers
living in our heads are doing.

We must wonder: How is it we can evolve so many complex things and not be able to evolve a fully conscious bio-computer? Something may not be right with this picture. Yes, we must at least wonder.

If my asking these questions suggests this is fantasy or science fiction-like material, Readers are invited to play this line of thinking out along those lines. If considering these ideas as fiction works for you, please then do think of this discussion as fantasy or science fiction. The mind is still considering the issues being raised on these pages.

If it does sound foolish to question evolution or intelligent design or both, if it sounds foolish to ask the questions I ask, we may want to ask ourselves what programming is causing us to take such monumental wonderings so lightly.

Remember, the brain, its executive control function operating you, is telling you this sounds like fantasy and fiction. (Take a moment, Reader, and say hello to the ECF for me. Perhaps tell your ECF you can see it there. Begin a dialog with this presence.)

At this point, some of my Readers tell me that, after all, control over the complex Human Brain should be done by higher powers, gods, or something higher than we simple Humans, that we are not fit to do this for ourselves. Again, I respond that turning control of our own awareness over to outside (or deeply buried unconscious) forces is not assuming our rightful control over what we know and *how we access what we know.*

Nor is turning control of our own awareness over to unseen mental functions something we necessarily would have chosen to be coded to do. Sure, we evolved or were designed to have this **not knowing function**, this not being fully conscious of all brain activity function, and we likely do well to dare to wonder why.

Think of our brains as our own personal library where we should be able to go to check out clearly indexed information when needed. However, for some reason, our brain's executive librarian has made it virtually impossible for us to

access everything that is in there, to know what all is available in our library.

But we own the library. We own the brain where the executive librarian works. We are in charge of deciding what information we can access, aren't we? Does the executive librarian report to us?

Not really.

Who is in charge here? Shouldn't we be allowed to be our own executive controlling us?

__Keep in mind, as we reason through this, that the executive running our thinking is watching us try to reason through this.__

__Would this executive want you to take yourself seriously when asking about all this?__

__This isn't some strange form of paranoia, this is an actual matter it is time we address.__

OUT FROM UNDER

It is time we move our own consciousness out from under control of the programmed-in, *implanted, executive* operating our thinking. Certainly, we can do this. Certainly our consciousness can take control, can rise above the control of our biological brain's absolute, automatic, unquestioned,

programmed-in control of us.

We must ask, who does our biological brain answer to? Us? Or? (As discussed in the first parts of this book and in other volumes in this series, we actually are both a physical lifeform, and also a non-physical, beyond simply biological, species of consciousness. We are the species of the Consciousness of Humanity. **We are far more than our biological brain and its executive control function running its thinking lets us know we are.**[59])

And there are still other Readers who say that we need our sub- and un- conscious brains to work silently, behind the scenes on the processes our brains engage in, to follow the coding and programming within them. This way we can do other things with our time, and avoid overload.

Again I say, of course avoiding overload is essential. However, we do know how to manage and organize information. We do not leave everything we have piled up on our desk tops at all times. (Think of your own office where you may leave your desk somewhat organized so that you can find what you need when you need it.)

The brain could be designed differently. And yes, of course, we have computers now, to do much of what our brains are

---

[59] See *Volume 3* in this series, *UNVEILING THE HIDDEN INSTINCT*, and the following book, *Volume 6* in this series, *OVERRIDING THE EXTINCTION SCENARIO, PART TWO*. Also see *Volume 10* in this series, *SEEING BEYOND OUR LINE OF SIGHT*.

not doing for us, although it is our brains who design these computers (at least so far).

Yet, these computers are not accessing the secrets our brains are not allowing us to know are there to access: *the truth about who and what and where we are,* **the information buried so deeply within our sub- and un- conscious.**

We have such magnificent brains with such powerful executive control functions. And after all, if these are OUR functions, then we have a right to be fully aware of what these are doing to and with us. We have a right to consciously use these functions as we consciously choose to.

After all, can we really say what of our brain's functions we should not be able to consciously access? Can we really say that without knowing what life with a *fully actuated brain* would be like?

How do we know what we are capable of when we cannot CONSCIOUSLY access IN FULL what we are capable of?

CONTROL
QUESTIONS

So, what controls our complex brain and how did we get to be controlled by this?

What genetic, evolutionary, god-like, or otherwise intelligent design created blocks to our having full control of our own minds and consciousness-es, to all levels of these? Who or what has programmed in to us, implanted, blocks to our own continuum of consciousness?[60]

What kind of executive control function is implanted into our brain? What kind of brain function is this that walls us out of monitoring in full what it is doing there in our brains and why?

Yes, we are told we should not take on too much, not take on more than we can, so as not to overload ourselves, so as not to overtax our brain's intra- and inter-cellular synaptic systems.

Really?

Is this actually true? Is this limited brain capacity honestly selected for, limited by evolution, for survival purposes?

Is it actually true that…

- with all that brain space we do not access on a conscious level;
- with all that brain we carry in our heads, not being consciously used by our conscious

---

[60] Refer to *Volume 10* in this series, titled, *SEEING BEYOND OUR LINE OF SIGHT*, for definition of, and discussion regarding accessing, this *continuum of consciousness.*

minds;
* with all that brain that belongs to us;

...that if this is really OUR own brain sitting there in our own head, we should just agree not to have full access to it?

Should we not
question
the design here?

Is it true that we should not, and cannot, find a way to access more of our own power of knowing and processing and organizing information?[61] Yes, of course "modern" Earth science is trying. However, we are taking the long path to something that is right here right now for us to access: *US*. Could we have been designed differently so this path to *US* would be ready and instant and always consciously accessible to *US*?

Think of a child of a wealthy parent. This child has been willed wealth for life, but has been willed wealth with controlled access to this wealth. Where there may or may not

---

[61] Certainly, science has provided us with the technology to have external hard drives and other mechanisms to allow our biological brains to extend their functions beyond their biology. While of course we are all benefitting from such developments (although these must also be closely monitored), we are not further determining our own programming, coding, and any external control of us, by engaging in technological extensions of ourselves and our brain power.

be good reasons for this in the case of material wealth ...

...what can we say about giving the Human Brain such great potential but limiting conscious access to this potential--while telling us this is for our own good, that we cannot handle what we would have access to?

Or is there another reason for this blocking of our full conscious access to our own library of ourselves?

What might we find out once we start asking?

αΩα

SECTION FOUR

Raising The Bar

On Our Own Evolution

αΩα

14
CAN OUR BRAIN
RAPIDLY
ADAPT ITSELF?

However we got here, however we "evolved" to this point, who or whatever did this to us or for us, or within us, we do not have to stay this way. *We can choose to consciously adapt, to* **meta-adapt***, to ever new levels of use of ourselves and our brains and our minds, our awareness-es, our consciousness-es.*

We can choose to purposefully evolve far more expansive aspects of ourselves. We can choose to see what is really going on, what is really happening to us, and do something about this.

ADAPTING

Our brains and minds can ever more consciously adapt themselves to address *their own increasing demands for control of their own functions, as well as control of their own territory, of their own continuum of consciousness.*

Our brains can adapt themselves toward greater and more conscious awareness of themselves. (This is going to be far more conscious awareness than currently practiced by meditative and or otherwise achieved "states" some say offer

full access to everything, to the oneness or some essence of existence such as prana.)

While the value of a meditative state is certainly present in many practices, here in this book, I am talking about achieving fully conscious, full and fully direct, unmediated access to our own mind, and more so, to our own consciousness itself.

RECOGNIZING
OUR
THOUGHT PROCESSING
HIERARCHIES AND FUNCTIONS

We are told and have no reason to doubt that, it is over time, over epochs, that our mind/brain has evolved an organizational hierarchy with an executive control function (ECF). In so doing, our brain has evolved a means of not only prioritizing use of, but even controlling our awareness of, *what we think, what we are allowed to think, and what we can know of what we think.*

This executive control function controlling the thoughts of our biological brain, controlling our thoughts, is working right now, perhaps to organize, and even filter, the ideas I am sharing on these pages, perhaps to be sure ...

> **we are not free thinking enough to**
> **fully wrap our minds around**
> **what is said in the paragraph above.**

OUR RIGHT TO FULL
AND CONSCIOUS USE
OF OUR OWN BRAINS

We Humans are exhibiting at least some awareness that we can benefit by bringing at least some of what is running deep inside our brains, under the radar, taking place in our sub- and un- conscious realms, into our awake, aware, conscious consciousness. We may not see exactly why we are drawn into these matters, however we are. In these "modern" times, this awareness is emerging into our educational, psychological, biological, and neurological sciences. (Yes, religion and various other practices have addressed these matters in their own ways for even longer.)

Note the relatively modern concept, "metacognition." The notion of metacognition has emerged in recent decades among scientists and educators. Our current views of metacognition are basically this: metacognition offers strategies for problem solving and learning, even for thinking about thinking where this assists in learning.

While the understanding and application of metacognition has thus far been primarily focused on learning and related cognitive activities, as per my discussion in this and the following books, I find there is much more to be said about this.

I say that metacognition is a still to be fully utilized powerful

tool that involves our being more and more, ever more, *conscious of our own thinking processes so as to direct them, so as to gain more and more conscious control of them.* I emphasize that the great value of an ever more in depth, ever more powerful, form of metacognition is ...

... learning more about and engaging in an advanced form of metacognition, or perhaps better stated, meta-meta-cognition (such as the *conscious metacognition* and *hyper-metacognition* I have developed for the work of detecting what is really going on in our own minds, as I define further in books listed at the end of this present book).

This **meta-cognitive awareness** can allow us to reach into that executive control function lurking in the brain. We can teach ourselves to reach in and take ever more *aware* conscious control over ever more key thinking activities of our brains. And this is just the start of what we can do as we learn to...

GO
EVER MORE
CONSCIOUS.

Over the years, I have conducted a series of studies with children who were taught to be aware of their thinking processes. Of the children I taught about thinking, about thinking about thinking, about learning to learn, about metacognition, back when they were ages three to ten, I have found that now, years later, many of them use this term, metacognition, today and are fully aware of what it means to

be aware of, or as several of these persons now describe this, to "think about my brain's thinking."

In fact, several have insisted that their schooling, and even life success so far in their adulthood, relates in some way to their heightened awareness of their own mental processes, of their own thinking, of their own information intake and processing functions, of their own brains and minds.

And this is just a small part of the access to our brains' executive control functioning that I say we have a right to.

What might it mean to have **heightened consciously aware control** *of our own bio-computers that we carry within us, of our own brains? Do we really want this thing we call our brain to control us without our being able to be highly aware of and involved in this control at any moment we may need to be? Do we really want to blindly submit to control without a highly aware conscious say in how we are being controlled and the various workings of this control?*

> **Throughout Human history on this Earth,**
> **many revolutions have been fought**
> **by peoples wanting**
> **to free themselves of**
> **the dictatorial, autocratic,**
> **political control**
> **they were being subjected to.**
> **They wanted**
> **more say**
> **in their own lives.**

Not yet have we Humans
sought to overturn the control over us
that our own brains,
and the genetic coding
directing our own brains to control us, have.

Why not?

Could our own brains be
genetically programmed to
block us from realizing
that our own brains,
and the coding wiring our brains,
have so much control over us that
we are not consciously seeing
what we are involved in?

Should we really just accept this situation,
even appreciate it as
convenient, logical, and best for us,
as a positive product of random evolution,
one naturally selecting
the "fittest" characteristics
to form the "fittest" species?

Should we really believe that
our brain's control over us,
was "selected" or evolved for us
via a natural process such as
this thing we call natural selection?

IS OUR BIOLOGICAL BRAIN
TOO ANTIQUATED?

The implications of our taking truly aware conscious control of our own thought prioritization and organization are indeed many. Can we do this? Do we have the brain capacity to do this? Is there a way to avoid overload?

Were we able to realize we can do this, and were we then willing to do this, we would experience a profound *leap* in our evolution, one we would have most purposefully aware and consciously brought about.

Yes, it has been suggested that this would place a tremendous burden on our biological brain. Yet, to this matter of this tremendous burden I say: this could be a tremendous burden *only upon what we are told are the supposedly limited (in terms of capacity) biological neural pathways we are presently using.*

Think of a large library full of books. You are not presented with these books all in a jumble, in a big pile on the floor. You are presented with a complete catalog that lets you see all that is there, and to search for and then access what you want and need on an as needed basis.

PROGRAMMED
NOT TO KNOW?

What if we are *programmed not to know* we can consciously aware and purposefully use far more of our brain's capacity

than we are allowed to know we can? What if we have *far greater capacity for awareness*, far more we can be aware of while we use it?

**What if our programming is designed
to restrict our awareness
for reasons other than protection
from overload?**

When we are able to take highly aware control of our own thought organizing metacognitive processes, we will be freeing ourselves from the invisible control of our programming, and of our programming to be programmable.

We will be freeing ourselves from the invisible (rather than conscious access to the) executive control function invisibly dictating what we know and are allowed to know, and are allowed to know we know.

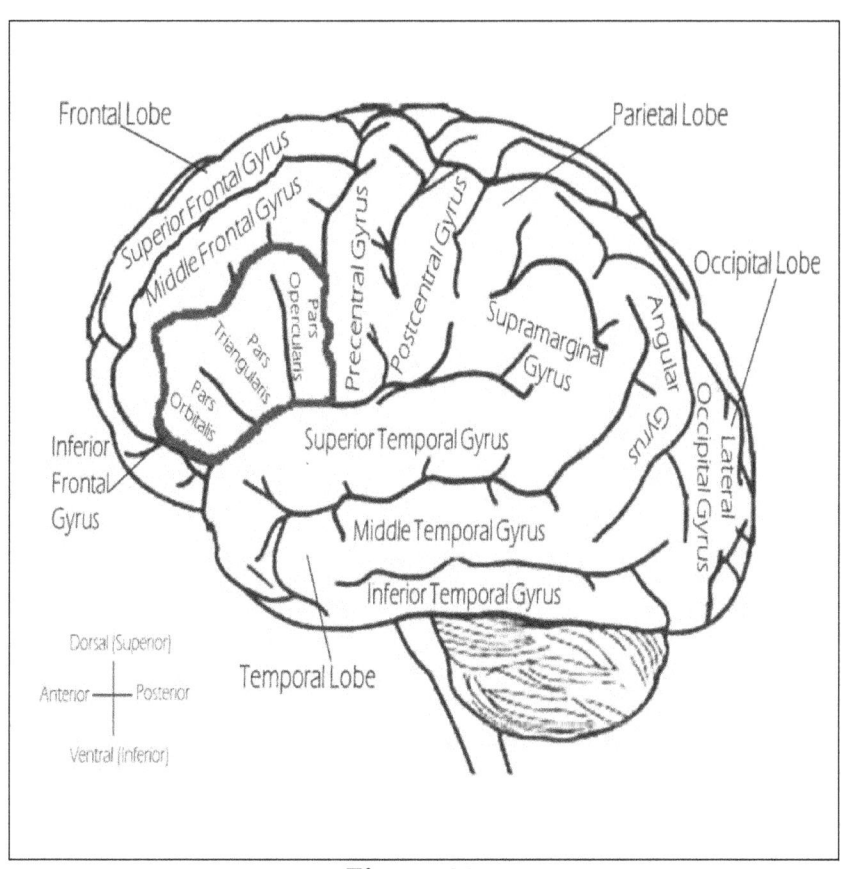

Figure 20:
Biological Brain Humans Carry
courtesy of Au.gov

αΩα

15
HUMAN SPECIES SURVIVAL BEYOND THIS ENDANGERED NICHE

Let's return to the matter of survival. Indeed, we are on a long journey of some form of evolution, of OUR evolution. Whether this evolution is divinely inspired, or directed by some other form of (intelligent) design, or a purely random "naturally selected" development and progression, or has been conducted in some other way, it is some form of process.

Evolution is an easy term to toss around, to apply where we wish to apply it. Yet, what this evolution really is, and how this evolution itself came to be, has not been absolutely proven beyond all doubt. Even classical natural selection theory itself has been debated, adjusted, revised, over time. (Note that Charles Darwin's own classical theory of evolution was proposed before genes were discovered.)

Some modern views include the argument that each evolutionary innovation has made it possible for greater complexity to arise. These views suggest that the emergence or evolution of biological complexity was more than simply the result of random natural selection, and or of random mutation.

Yet, however evolution has developed or propelled itself, its very existence, let alone its purpose, must at least be questioned:

WHO OR WHAT DESIGNED EVOLUTION ITSELF?

CAN WE BE CERTAIN EVOLUTION ITSELF
WAS A RANDOM AND NATURAL DEVELOPMENT?

WHO WROTE THIS SCRIPT?

THIS IS OUR OWN EVOLUTION TO OWN

However we view this evolution our species is apparently engaged in, this is OUR evolution, isn't it? We believe this is *our* evolution, yet might we want to ask whether this is truly *us evolving ourselves, or some other factor or intelligence so doing*?

Again, what I am asking is, if this is indeed evolution we are in the process of, whose evolution is this? Who designed this evolution? Is evolution itself simply a random or even accidental happening in the cosmos, or something ordained by holy or other higher powers or intelligences?

And how intelligent is the designer of this evolution (if this is indeed an intelligently designed process) given that so many species fail to thrive, even die out?

Or is *species die out*, extinction, purposefully part of the intelligently designed process? If so, why?

Why design a process that allows a species to come into being and to then die out?

Is this *extinction test* necessary? Why not design species to survive even changing climate, geological, geo-political, and other environments?[62]

CROSS SPECIES SHARED EVOLUTION?

Of course, if this evolution is merely a random event occurring with no intelligent or even divine designer behind it, would this explain any better how the "natural" selection process includes species die out, extinction? Why not design us to access the actual survival awareness-es we carry so deeply within us?

If we assume the fittest species survives while another species dies out, this may mean that we are really talking about the survival of the *fittest species*. Are species evolved, selected, to fail to survive because this is the *selection of the fittest among a group of species* rather than within any one individual species?

We of course must ask whether we may actually be talking about the survival of groups of species, of groups of life forms sharing a biological (or other) niche.

---

[62] Yes, we are trying to survive the changing environment we face on Earth. However, our adaptation process is perhaps limited by what we have so far evolved and not evolved into ourselves regarding consciously enhanced, or what I call conscious meta- adaptation, capability.

There are many ways to see what is happening. Ultimately, these are questions we must ask, questions we have a right to ask. Yet, the full extent and detail of these questions we may not know to ask, as our brains may not be programmed to let us ask. Nevertheless, these are questions that can help us open our minds and detect what is happening to us.

SO, ARE WE EARTH HUMANS SIMPLY LAB RATS IN AN EXTINCTION EXPERIMENT?

Can we proceed as we have been once we dare to ask:

Are we Human Beings on Earth subjects in some kind of *extinction experiment* being conducted by some force or factor or intelligence far greater than ourselves?

Could there be an intelligence driving, designing, the natural and or other selection processes?

The truth is, once we step back from our belief systems and sciences, we simply do not know. Yet, we must dare to ask.

All this being said, it makes sense for us to own our own evolution, even to take command of it now.

We can indeed own this journey, we can indeed take charge of, take increasing control of, this journey — of our evolution itself. We can indeed come to terms with the possibilities

examined on these pages, if for no other reason than to raise our awareness of possible directions for our future evolution.

Where we have the option of understanding ourselves as *life forms of consciousness, members of a species of consciousness,* who happen to be living in physical biological bodies on 3-D Planet Earth at this time, we might see *how interdimensional our evolution can and must be.*

Our understanding of who we are is here for us. We can choose to recognize ourselves as beings who can move back and forth, to and from, in and out of, physicality, who can be both physicalized and non-physicalized at the same time.

Once we see this, then it is natural for us to expand ourselves along our own ***continuum of consciousness*** where we already do exist, and where we can survive.[63]

Readers, no matter what your particular beliefs and sciences are telling you about all this, no matter what your beliefs regarding how we arrived here, we are at this powerful moment in our existence, this potentially perilous time in our physical Earth niche existence.

To survive: *we can and must shift, heighten, our level of conscious awareness of our evolution options so as to further engage in our determination our own fate.*

---

[63] See definition and discussion of this **continuum of consciousness** in other books in this *KEYS TO CONSCIOUSNESS AND SURVIVAL SERIES*, especially *Volume 10*, titled, *SEEING BEYOND OUR LINE OF SIGHT.*

We can and must understand that our survival is, yes, about the survival of each of us and our own offspring—and is also about the survival of our species—and of our species of consciousness which is actually who we are.

We know this. We feel this in our hearts. We want our families, friends, communities, all those we care about and identify with, to survive. Even more so, we want our species to survive.

We are the Human Species and we want to survive. Don't we?

YES, SPECIES SURVIVAL

We as a population of Humans living on Earth are coming to see that our survival is indeed a species survival. Of course, we have always been aware of this; however, much of what Humans do focuses more specifically on themselves and their own offspring.

We would like to believe that over time we progress further toward the ability to survive. Most Humans would like to see our species evolve better and better means of surviving, yes?

After all, we think, *what is our evolution if not the process of*

surviving, and of optimizing our survival—and of doing an ever better job of this over time?

(However, we are not necessarily able to say we are doing an ever better job of surviving. After all, we have ever changing survival pressures that we may not see in full. So how can we know until far later in time whether we are doing an ever better job of surviving today?)

Can we, will we, survive into the future to look back at now and know whether we succeeded in furthering the survival of our species? <u>Will we still exist to ask?</u>

At this time in our history and or evolution, we do see, more and more so, that we are doing this evolving together, that we are evolving as a species, even as groups of species, even as a biosphere. This evolution is therefore about all of us. This survival is about all of us.

WE ARE A LIFE FORM, A FORM OF LIVING CONSCIOUSNESS

We can rethink who we are. Our species itself is a life form. However, here on Earth living as biological animals, we tend to focus on who we are as *biological individuals* to such an extent that we miss so much of our identity as both a physical and a non-physical species. We may be missing so much of our identity as a *species of consciousness.*

Still, we are living as both our individual and our collective life form. And we are living as both individual consciousness

and our collective consciousness. *We are life forms, yes, we are life forms of consciousness.*

As the species that we are, we are part of one life form, this Human life form. We are somewhat like a jelly fish, an animal which is itself a colony of jelly fish cells living together, needing each other to survive. As such, we are a colony of Human Beings living together, needing each other to survive here on Earth.

Our needing each other to survive is complex, as this survival is something we want to do here on Earth in this particular physical plane niche, yes. And, I say here, this survival is something we also want to do BEYOND this particular niche, and BEYOND this particular dimension. We want to be SEEING BEYOND now, to see how vast our realities are. (See *Volume 10* in this series, *SEEING BEYOND OUR LINE OF SIGHT*, for more discussion of this matter.)

This survival involves our understanding who we are as a species ...

> **... and how much momentum our species can have toward its expanded levels of survival.**

As individuals and as a species, we know only what we can know, *what our biological brains allow us to know.* And, of what we know, we believe we know what we know. Yet, while we allow our biological brains to control all information we recognize, process, and use, we know less than we can know.

We tend to know only what our brains tell us we think or feel we know and need to know.

We, both as individuals and also as a species, know only what our biological brains allow us to know. We do not consciously know all we and our species know, however our brain knows much of what it blocks our conscious mind from knowing.

**We Humans know
more than
we know ourselves to know.**

**On some level,
we Humans do know we are living
along our continuum of consciousness,
although full awareness of this is
not allowed into
our conscious awareness
by our biological brains.
Our biological brains are coded,
programmed,
to wall out the
vastness of our continuum,
to block this from our awareness,
and thus to block our
full access.**

To truly survive, we must consciously have access to all we can know, and all we have been evolved, coded, or programmed not to see we can know.

We can and do know more than we allow ourselves (or are allowed) to know, more than we know we can know, more than we feel we need to know to survive here and everywhere else we can live. This is all quite simple although seemingly somewhat complex in that this is a slightly different approach to our knowing what we have a right to know.

ASSUMING CONTROL OVER
OUR RECOGNITION
AND USE OF INFORMATION

As a species, we can and must assume control over the flow of information into our awareness, over the recognition of information coming to us and within us. We can choose to become far more conscious of important information than we are allowed to be. We can take control of our biological brain's control of us. We can take conscious control of our brain's control of itself. *We can take over what has taken us over.*

We can decide what it is we do need to know to survive, to truly survive. Actually, we can even decide for ourselves what it is that we want to mean by the survival of our species.

This is about reaching past limits on our perceptions, on our consciousness-es, past limits that have been biologically evolved, implanted, into us. So, our understanding of our survival is presently based on what we feel is our survival, what we have been led to believe are the boundaries of our survival.

While it is indeed essential we survive in this physical niche here on this Earth, we must be allowed to see other opportunities and options for survival *in case we need these.* Other options for survival may at some point be very necessary for us, for us to actually survive as a species. Our survival may require that we know more of what we need to know, that we realize what we need to know is more than we, our brains, are consciously accessing at this present time.

We need to know a great deal about our range of survival options, and we need to do this knowing *now,* and on multiple levels. Even our Human biological brains, which have been *programmed to limit our conscious knowing,* can be freed to allow more knowing, can indeed do this expanded and conscious knowing, although these brains of ours have been wired not to do so, not to allow key information into our conscious awareness...

... even not to allow key survival information into our conscious awareness.

This coded-in filtering out of key information is a threat to our survival. Although we cannot know what all we are blocked from accessing, being unable to access the information we carry within ourselves, being unable to know whether we are carrying essential information, is itself counter survival.

Accessing our own interdimensional awareness is essential.

Even our biological brains can be released from the shackles of trapping neurobiological and biochemical blocks to knowing, from embedded blocks resulting from our programming. We can be liberated from coded-in controls so as to help liberate our species from controls we do not need to carry.

On some level, we all know that the Human Mind—and its Human Consciousness—can now, and must now, evolve more rapidly than does the Human Biology.

This means that the Human Brain itself may need to ever more consciously perceive the situation, the reality, and to indeed *evolve itself far more rapidly than does general Human Biology*, including the Human Brain. Is this brain programmed to allow this?

This is clearly about having our Human Consciousness, who we truly are, take control of our evolution on Earth (and beyond), instead of the reverse which has so far been the case here on Earth.

Our niches expand well into the realm of our consciousness, a domain we have been allowed only limited conscious access to by our biology, by our biological brain. We have been programmed to be restricted from our own continuum of

consciousness, our own territory, our true niche.[64]

HUMAN MIND
HAS BEEN
BLOCKED FROM KNOWING

It is the Human Brain itself that can call our attention (yet generally opts not to call our attention) to our situation at this time. It is the physical biological Human Brain that reveals, upon close examination, our wiring, our programming, programming that holds us to a near standstill relative to the speed at which we have a right to evolve. I do say a *right to evolve* here, as I maintain that we have been biologically evolved in this Earth niche with, designed with, implanted with, blocks to knowing all this—even blocks to our interdimensional evolutionary potential.

The so-called natural selection process has inhibited, blocked, our knowing key survival information.

Again I ask, would a species block itself from full access to itself? Would a species block itself from full access to the survival-related information and capability it carries deep within itself?

Why wouldn't a life form who is designed to survive allow itself full access to all it may need to know to survive? Why wouldn't a life form allow itself full access to its own niche, its own continuum of consciousness?

---

[64] See again *Volume 10* titled, *SEEING BEYOND OUR LINE OF SIGHT.*

IS IT POSSIBLE OUR LIFE FORM
WAS NOT DESIGNED TO SURVIVE?

IS IT POSSIBLE THIS
BLOCKING OF ACCESS TO OUR ACTUAL NICHE,
TO OUR CONTINUUM OF CONSCIOUSNESS,
IS CENTRAL IN THE SPECIES EXTINCTION TRIAL
WE ARE SUBJECTS IN?

QUESTION
PROGRAMMED-IN
NOT KNOWING

Do we really accept that this *form* of not knowing, this lack of access to information *trait*, was selected for in a survival of the fittest process? Is this not knowing, not accessing, ourselves, really the product of evolution?

Or is this the control imposed upon us by the *species extinction trial* we have been subjected to?

There are many ways of explaining what it is that controls or directs us here on this biological Earth niche level, or even at the interdimensional or what some will choose to call the cosmic or divine level. Addressing this matter is a complex discussion that will relate to Readers' own belief systems and can be cast in many different directions.

Again, I say that no matter what a Reader's belief system,

whatever a Reader chooses to say these controlling forces may be—even if these forces are simply a randomly misguided biological evolution and nothing more—we must take heed of our situation now.

No matter how we explain the presence of these forces, we must take heed of the limitations our physical plane biological Earth Human Brains have implanted within themselves, the blocks to our knowing what is really going on, to our being fully conscious *and capable of being fully conscious*, of information relevant to our survival.

We may have to know more now—if we choose to survive, that is.

PROGRAMMED TO BLOCK KNOWING BY BEING FORCED TO STAY TRAPPED IN KNOWING LESS

These blocks to fully knowing are designed to function via programmed-in or implanted *addictions to less than fully perceived realities*. We get locked in to believing that what we can do, what we can know, where we can go, is what we think it is.

We get locked into believing we are who we think we are, we are who our biological brain tells us we are, and that we are limited in the ways our biology says we are.

(Of course, our physical plane limitations are definite and

even necessary here, as we are living in physical bodies. However, it is time for us to fully claim our understanding of ourselves as living concurrently in both physicality, and at the same time, along the inter-dimensional continuum, with the inter-dimensional matrix, of our consciousness which is our actual niche.[65])

We are blocked via our biological brain's programming, blocked from fully perceiving a more expansive perspective. We are being profoundly limited via our programming.

Again and again this is the question: Could the Human Brain be limited for some reason? Could this brain be blocked for some purpose? Was all of this simply evolutionary accident? Some kind of random development or lack thereof?

Could the shackles of our brain's programming be implanted within us to control us, to hold us captive in our definition of ourselves as only a physical plane biological Earth species?

Or, is there something other than this that can explain what is going on here? Is it that our biological Human Brain is now antiquated, that it is no longer enough to take us where we need to go and to tell us what we need to know to survive? Is the Human Brain archaic? Is this archaic condition a natural (naturally selected) or planned (perhaps designed)

---

[65] Explore further this continuum and this matrix in other volumes in this series, such as *Volume 3*, titled, *UNVEILING THE HIDDEN INSTINCT*, and *Volume 10*, titled, *SEEING BEYOND OUR LINE OF SIGHT.*

obsolescence?

Is what we are able to access of our Human Brain itself archaic? Can we reach around the biological block programmed into us? Can we consciously release and gain full access to our awareness and consciousness functions? Will we be allowed to do this? What or who will allow us? Will our biological programming say no?

SEEDS OF
OUR GREATER POTENTIAL
ARE HERE

I say that the seeds of our greater Human Potential are embedded within us, and that, the keys to this potential are stored away, or locked away. It is as if we are locked in to this level of knowing and to this level of being for some reason perhaps not of our own choice, or not of our fully conscious choice.

Of course, for those who say this is simply the result of our evolution, of how our biological Human Bodies and Human Brains evolved here on Earth, I again say maybe, perhaps. However, if this is the explanation for our situation, then I say it is time we take conscious control over our own evolution, time we assume conscious control of who we are and of who we are able to become as a species of consciousness.

It is time we REVOLT against the limiting coding that we carry within our own genetics. I return again to the concept of REVOLTAS I share earlier in this book:

R = revolutionary
E = evolution
V = vesting
O = ourselves in
L = lateral and
T = transmigratory
A = awareness and
S = survival

REVOLTAS
SURGIS

However we have arrived in this situation, are we simply carriers of our brain's (or some higher level's) executive control programming which limits us, which addicts us:

> to beliefs we (are programmed to) have
> in the realities we think we inhabit;

> to beliefs we (are programmed to) have
> regarding the boundaries of what we inhabit; and,

> to beliefs (we are programmed to) have
> regarding who we think we are?

Who are we as Human Beings today? Or, who do we think we Human Beings are today? Don't we want to know? Don't we have a right to know? What blocks are there to our truly knowing and why?

[How can we break through these limitations and do so now? How can we be certain that any belief systems or practices or drugs we are offered (claiming that these can raise our consciousness-es, or protect or save us) are not also themselves *filtering our awareness-es*, directing us down their own alleys with their own (philosophical or biochemical) agendas? **Direct access to ourselves is direct when actually direct rather than the result of electro-biochemically determined cognitive and or emotional detours.**]

How can we find out if the boundaries to our existence are the actual boundaries, or boundaries we have somehow accepted or been programmed to accept to hold us captive, to keep us and our awareness-es under control?

Can we set ourselves, the captives of implanted controls on our awareness, free?

αΩα

16
THIS HUMAN BRAIN
MUST SEE THROUGH ITS CONSTRAINTS

Let's dig deeper here. The frontal area (generally the prefrontal cortex) of the biological Human Brain contains the cells, the neurons, that regulate emotions as well as conduct what "modern" brain scientists have described as the "executive" functioning described throughout this book.

This executive control function (ECF) controls what are considered the Human Brain's "higher level" processes such as: self awareness, attention, organization, planning, self-monitoring, abstract reasoning, problem solving, decision making, mental flexibility, the capacity to use external clues to govern behavior, and other relatively complex processes.

And yes, the prefrontal cortex of the biological Human Brain is some 120 percent larger than that brain area in other primate organisms living on Earth. This size advantage is (presumably) giving the Human Animal what are its so-called "higher intellectual functions." Of course, these so-called higher intellectual functions are higher functions in terms of what we biological Humans with biological Human Brains are told by our biological brains we value, what we consider top of the line mental capabilities, higher than what we believe any other mammal (or other animal) carries. Of

course, we cannot know what higher order functions may be taking place in other life forms' brains, as we can only detect these based on what our own brain tells us.

I do have to ask here whether we also believe that these so-called "higher" intellectual functions are higher not only than those of other animals here on Earth, but higher than those of any other possible life forms or intelligences anywhere in this cosmos. (And yes, some of my Readers and audience members have told me that of course these are not higher than God's functions, which are supreme, but are higher than any other life God has created here. I leave this matter of God to my Readers to decide.)

I do ask whether there could be any other higher intelligences out there as well, any others whose intellectual functions surpass those of we Biological Humans here on Earth.

Do we not at least have to wonder: who or what had the capacity to program us, to code us, to design or otherwise evolve us the way we have been?

In other words, if there is a Godly or other higher intelligence out there, might we be the product of that higher intelligence's INTELLIGENT DESIGN? And if so, might the limits on our evolution and mental capacity also be the product of that intelligent design?

If so, then allow me to simply wonder here, how benevolent is an intelligent design that limits us so as to keep us from CONSCIOUSLY accessing all we can know about who, what, and where we actually are.

After all, if a Godly or other intelligent designer developed or evolved or created us, that designer likely had the power to give us: full access to our own minds; fully aware full access to our own <u>continuum of consciousness</u>; as well as the power to generate within us a far higher level of awareness--but apparently did not design us with these accesses to ourselves.

WE HUMANS
NEED TO KNOW MORE

Given the discussion I offer in this book, it is rather clear that the apparent higher intellectual functions of we Earth Humans are perhaps not as high as we may need to have them be TO SURVIVE.

As noted above, our higher intellectual functions are mostly conducted in the frontal area of our Human Brain, where our brain's executive control functions are largely based. Be sure to note the term "control" in this label for our seeming higher functions: executive CONTROL functions.

Again and again, we must dare to ask: Could control of we biological Earth Humans be what this executive function is actually about? Consider the possibility that the more advanced a prison system gets, the more it can place control

of the prisoners within the prisoners. Actual bars become a thing of the past. This is not to say we Humans are prisoners, but this is to say we must wonder whether we are captives of some form, perhaps of our own programming.

This and the following *OVERRIDING THE EXTINCTION SCENARIO* book (Part Two) offer a new perspective on the current limits of our biological brain, especially on its frontal area. **This frontal area of our brain is captive of the genetic coding that created it and of the programming the coding codes for, and of the neural wiring the programming develops and operates through.**

αΩα

17
WALKING THIS EARTH
OR BETTER STATED,
THIS CONTINUUM WHERE WE LIVE

We Humans have been walking this Earth for many millennia, have traveled through time and history to be here today. This in itself is a magnificent journey. We have come so far. I say nothing to discredit or devalue the profound journey our time on this Earth has been and continues to be. I do, however, have to question what our evolution is actually all about.

Even in our "modern" times, our bodies and brains continue to function, in so many ways, according to hunting and gathering needs appropriate to our existence on this Earth thousands of years and longer ago. Processes formerly necessary for our basic safety and survival may now still be necessary, yet not necessary as much or in the same ways they were needed when life was more outdoor-based and less protected from other animals and the elements.

OTHER FORMS OF
PREDATORS

Today we face other forms of predators, other and or different forms of the elements, and other dangers our conscious

251

brains may not be coded to consciously detect in full or at all, let alone to adequately if at all respond to. Perhaps we have to stop a moment, and allow ourselves, dare ourselves, to ask these BIG questions....

Is the Human Brain truly fully prepared
to live in these "modern" times,
in this "modern" and changing,
perhaps even deteriorating,
biospheric Earth niche?

And if not,
why not?

And once we ask these questions, we may have to also allow ourselves to ask these FAR BIGGER QUESTIONS....

How would we know, were we not prepared to know?

How would we know,
were we not
fully prepared to live in these times,
to SURVIVE in these and the coming times?

How do we know whether we can survive
the changing and perhaps
deteriorating of our Earth niche?
HOW?
HOW?
HOW?

Our still running old biological brains, which may have served us rather well during earlier stages of our time or evolution here on physical plane Earth, may now be working "for" us at cross purposes.

In other words, our old biological brain and its programming may be *failing to respond* to emerging survival pressures by not allowing us access to our own full range of information, to our own full range of consciousness. This is information we may need to have to survive in these and coming times.

I say "may be failing to respond" here. However, the question is: is our brain simply failing to respond, or is our brain actually *programmed to fail to respond, programmed to block our full access* to the consciousness we carry so deeply within ourselves?

Our old brains may be holding us back from knowing all we need to and actually can know. Our old brains may be keeping us from using these very brains in full, from using all we have to work with, employing all these brains themselves are capable of—or all we, who we truly are, our consciousness-es themselves, are actually capable of.

Our old minds themselves are so much more capable than they seem to know themselves to be on a conscious level, and thus are less than fully activated and actuated.

And where we are more than our biological brains, we are limited by our biological brains from fully knowing who we are and what we can do.

Note: Yes, again, about here when I present this material, those among my audience members who believe that religion, and or meditation, and or psychoactive drugs, etc., can be paths to fully knowing, speak up. And their comments are good to listen to. However, I do believe these views are not quite hearing me. Awareness of the one-ness is yes, a form of enlightenment; however, this is not full conscious control of the brain, this thing that lives in our heads and runs us, controls us, limits us according to coding we have either evolved or been implanted with.

So here in this book, I am not advocating moving into an altered state several steps away from full and direct, unmediated, access to our consciousness to know and see more. I am talking about being fully conscious while we fully know all we can know.

Fully appreciating some altered states for what these may offer, I want to be clear here: *the introduction of other than ourselves into ourselves does not take us to ourselves, rather to the biological brain's experience of our biological selves under the influence of that which is not ourselves.*[66]

OUR OLD BRAINS MAY BE UNAWARE
THAT WE CAN HAVE CONSCIOUS CAPACITY
TO FUNCTION CONSCIOUSLY
ON A VERY VERY HIGH LEVEL

---

[66] An altered state is not the state of ourselves, rather it is a state of our altered selves. Watch for the illusion of self that many altered states offer.

Our old-model biological brains are largely unaware of themselves, largely run unaware (at least on a conscious level) that they are running, existing. Our biological brains do not consciously know what they are doing, and do not consciously know of their own potential. These biological brains of ours are not consciously aware of what may be blocking them, or inhibiting them, from utilizing their own potential.

Our old-model biological brains who are not fully aware of themselves are not consciously able to detect what may be blocking or controlling their access to themselves.

They are therefore not seeing what wiring or programming (however this programming was implanted or coded or both) inhabits us via our brain's executive control functions. Instead, our old brains allow us to run at diminished, not actuated, sub- (and sub-sub-) levels, compromising our own power, and frequently running at even quite dysfunctional (or what some describe as confused, disturbed, troubled, sick, addicted, etc.) levels.

OLD BRAIN FUNCTIONS
ARE BEING
EASILY MISAPPLIED

Here are some of the many old functions of our old biological brain that can be and are today too frequently being misapplied, misdirected, even corrupted:

- *Pleasure centers in the brain* which attract us to, and compel us to continue, particular survival-like behaviors such as consuming in excess or to an undesirable degree, food and/or compounds we intake as if they were food (alcohol, drugs, etc.);

- *Pleasure centers in the brain and their hormonal activation mechanisms* which attract us to, and compel us to mate with other Humans in order to reproduce, or to perform as if we are reproducing even when this is not the conscious intention of this behavior;

- *Activating, energizing, impulse response centers in the brain* that trigger readiness for, and even actual, impulse responses to events such as threats of danger, perceived danger, and actual danger, in which we prepare to move quickly to fight or take flight (and which frequently mis-react and mis-perform on impulse various violent acts against other persons who pose no actual danger).

These are evolved-in (and or implanted-in) ancient mechanisms that our brains are coded to program themselves for, so as to activate whenever triggered. We are fortunate that these mechanisms work virtually automatically, even to this day. We eat, reproduce, respond to danger, stop at red traffic lights without thinking, and so on because we are able to program and reward ourselves for such programming of

our brains.

Thanks to many of our biological brain's survival oriented mechanisms such as these listed above, we are successful ancient biological organisms surviving into these times. Yet, many of our biological brain functions, such as those listed above, are outdated and less than entirely functional for us in our world today. We engage in too many counter-survival behaviors as a result.

OLD BRAIN MISSING OUT ON IMPORTANT OPPORTUNITIES

Too frequently, these old basic survival functions are doing the opposite of helping us survive in these modern times.

> **The Human Brain may not have**
> **evolved quickly enough**
> **to adapt**
> **to the modern environment.**
> **Did our biological brain simply miss out**
> **on particular evolutionary opportunities,**
> **or was this brain prevented from**
> **realizing these opportunities?**

We do well to at least ask ourselves these questions, to at least wonder. So here we Humans are today, carrying around our old biological Human Brains that are:

- Brains that have implanted within them age old survival oriented mechanisms that are frequently

now in our modern times running awry, not always serving us in a positive or survival oriented way;

- Brains that are not able to consciously access all they take in and know while they often misread the information they are taking in;

- Brains that do not have conscious and full access to their own executive control functions;

- Brains that do not even know consciously when they are choosing to let some information into their awareness, and when they are choosing to wall some information out of their awareness;

- Brains that are not able to know in full what is there running them, directing them, controlling them, exactly what sort of mechanisms, codings, programmings, and or other control functions are at work within them;

- Brains that are not able to detect brain functions that are not in place via the brain's own choice, desire, and do not necessarily serve the brain's own survival—or the brain's own (or our own?) species' survival.

αΩα

18
WE CAN RAISE THE BAR

But what if we can raise the bar on our brains, break through the limits embedded in our brains and programming? What if we can free ourselves of the boundaries of our old brain's programmings?

Can we truly break free? What would this breaking free look like? These are questions we have a right to ask, and must be asking now.

WE CAN
BREAK FREE

Well, we *can* break free. We can discover, turn on, develop, nourish, *activate* our blocked and even our new mental capabilities. We can do this in a critical mass of, if not all of, our species' members. We have the knowledge and the tools to enhance the *awareness capacity of our species*.

WE MAY
HAVE BEEN
DESIGNED TO FALL PREY

We can begin by understanding that we are literally designed to fall prey to programming that holds us limited, and even

restricted, here in this physical plane niche **where we are told we live**.

We are held to this restricted view of who we are by our programming, by our biological brain's controlling system. We are in this sense, captives of the executive control function operating our brain, operating us, defining us as life forms of only this physical dimension on 3-D Earth, in this supposedly limited Human lifespan.

And the mechanism for controlling us, for keeping us running on an automatic level so that we are not able to see what controls us or that we are being controlled, is the biological wiring in our biological brain that renders us ever more readily programmable—readily put onto automatic tracks—habituated, addicted to our so-called perceptions, to our seeming boundaries, and to our behaviors within these.

**We are obedient beings,
believing what we are told by our brains.**

WE ARE
NOT ONLY
CREATURES OF HABIT

If we look closely, we can see that we are not only creatures of habit, but that we are frequently slaves to habits. We are guaranteed (as slaves to our own programming) not to see what is really taking place as per our brains, our minds, our species.

The following book, *OVERRIDING THE EXTINCTION SCENARIO, PART TWO*: *RAISING THE BAR ON THE EVOLUTION OF THE HUMAN SPECIES*, discusses some of the constraints implanted within our brains. I bring in scientific findings about our brains and show how these are actually indicating, to a stunning extent, what I am saying in these *OVERRIDING THE EXTINCTION SCENARIO* books.

We are on the long trek of evolution, or part of some process so much larger that we cannot see it for what it is. We must begin by DETECTING THE BAR ON THE EVOLUTION OF THE HUMAN SPECIES. Once we see what is happening here, we can begin to RAISE THE BAR ON THE EVOLUTION OF THE HUMAN SPECIES.

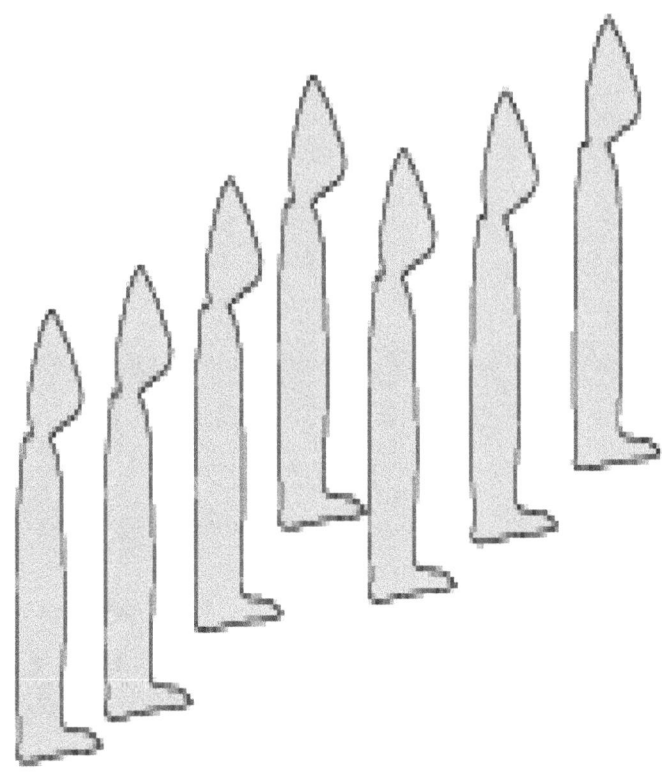

Figure 21.
The March Of Evolution
Into Other Niches And Other Dimensions

STAY TUNED FOR THE NEXT BOOK, WHERE DETAILS OF WHAT IS HAPPENING TO OUR BRAINS AND MINDS ARE EXPLORED....
AND WHERE OUR NEXT STEPS ARE SUGGESTED:

OVERRIDING THE EXTINCTION SCENARIO PART <u>TWO</u>:
<u>RAISING</u> THE BAR ON THE EVOLUTION OF THE HUMAN SPECIES.

The Eternal Journey

Wander on.
Realms, new realities
Having been here all along
Await.
Such a grand undertaking
Seeing this lifetime
Seeing this reality
As something the self can see
As it wishes.
Yet such a step it is along the epic journey
The quintessential pilgrimage
The honoring of self.
Crystalline windows
Clearer than clear
Pure vision beyond all seeing.
Rush of sensations beyond
The material plane.
Consciousness
Consciousness
Crystals of consciousness
Forming and unforming
Becoming more than they are
More than they have known themselves to be
More than here and now.
Consciousness reaching beyond illusion
Beyond already dissolving and dissolved limits
Because it already always can.

Angela Brownemiller

In The Words Of Others

Nirvana is not like the black,
dead peace of the grave,
but the living peace,
the living happiness of
a soul which is
conscious of itself,
and conscious of having found
its own abode in the heart of the
Eternal.

Mahatma Mohandas Karamchand Gandhi
All Religions are True

DETECTING THE BAR ON THE EVOLUTION OF THE HUMAN SPECIES

In The Words Of Others, continued....

If the doors of perception were cleansed, every thing would appear to man as it is, Infinite. For man has closed himself up, till he sees all things thro' narrow chinks of his cavern.

William Blake
The Marriage of Heaven and Hell

I regard consciousness as fundamental. I regard matter as derivative from consciousness. We cannot get behind consciousness. Everything that we talk about, everything that we regard as existing, postulates consciousness.

Max Planck
In The Observer, J. Fussell, Where is Science Going?

It seems to me what is called for is an exquisite balance between two conflicting needs: the most skeptical scrutiny of all hypotheses that are served up to us and at the same time a great openness to new ideas. Obviously those two modes of thought are in some tension. But if you are able to exercise only one of these modes, whichever one it is, you're in deep trouble.

Carl Sagan
The Burden of Skepticism

....biologists have become increasingly aware that epigenetic mechanisms can lead to phenotypic changes in the next generation through gametic transmission of epigenetic variations. The consequences of this for evolutionary thinking are profound, and the view of evolution that is now emerging is significantly different from the neo-Darwinian view that dominated evolutionary thought in the second half of the 20th century.

Eva Jablonka
Epigenetic Inheritance and Plasticity

With the advent of Human beings, evolution has ceased to be a blind affair governed by random genetic mutations. A new degree of freedom has appeared; we can think ahead and determine our own future.

Peter Russell
The Evolution of Consciousness

Metaxis: …the state of belonging completely and simultaneously to two different, autonomous worlds: the image of reality and the reality of the image.

Augusto Boal
Theatre of the Oppressed

A metalogue is a conversation about some problematic subject. This conversation should be such that not only do the participants discuss the problem but the structure of the conversation as a whole is also relevant to the same.

Gregory Bateson
Steps to An Ecology of Mind

Metaxu: Two prisoners whose cells adjoin communicate with each other by knocking on the wall. The wall is the thing which separates them but it is also their means of communication. It is the same with us and God. Every separation is a link.

Simone Weil
From Sean Steel, Pursuit of Wisdom and Happiness in Education

All Human beings, all persons who reach adulthood in the world today, are programmed biocomputers. None of us can escape our own nature as programmable entities.

John C. Lilly
Programming and Metaprogramming in The Human Biocomputer

When scientists muster the courage to face this evidence unflinchingly, the greatest superstition of our age — the notion that the brain generates consciousness or is identical with it — will topple. In its place will arise a nonlocal picture of the mind.

Larry Dossey
Why Consciousness is Not the Brain

The day science begins to study non-physical phenomena, it will make more progress in one decade than in all the previous centuries of its existence. To understand the true nature of the universe, one must think in terms of energy, *frequency, and vibration.*

Nikola Tesla
Quoted by Swami Vivekananda, Tesla's Mentor

Researchers using brain imaging techniques...can often deduce with a significant degree of success the general nature of the contents of a subject's consciousness from the anatomic and temporal distribution of neural activity generated in the subject's cortex.

Nancy Kanwisher
Functional Specificity in the Human Brain

According to Neural Darwinism, these forebrain structures were selected for during evolution because they allowed for the planning of adaptive behavior in a complex, changing environment.

Gerald Edelman
Neural Darwinism

We remain confounded by ... the inability to explain in scientific terms the phenomenal "feel" of conscious experience.

D. Chalmers
The Conscious Mind

APPENDICES

BOOKLIST AND RECOMMENDED READING
KEYS TO CONSCIOUSNESS AND SURVIVAL SERIES
by Dr. Angela Brownemiller:

Volume 10
Seeing Beyond Our Line of Sight
Consciously Moving Through Life's Changes, Transitions, and Deaths
****
Volume 9
Navigating Life's Stuff – Dynamics of Personal Change, Book Two
Keys to Consciously Moving Through Our Processes and Their Patterns
****
Volume 8
Navigating Life's Stuff – Dynamics of Personal Change, Book One
Sensitizing to and Navigating Our Patterns and Their Processes
****
Volume 7
The Go Conscious Process:
Steps and Practices for Heightening Conscious Awareness,
Shifts, Transmigrations of Focus, LEAPS OF SELF
****
Volume 6
Overriding the Extinction Scenario, Part Two:
Raising the Bar on the Evolution of the Human Species
****
Volume 5
Overriding the Extinction Scenario, Part One:
Detecting the Bar on the Evolution of the Human Species
****
Volume 4
How to Die and Survive:
Interdimensional Psychology, Consciousness,
and Survival: Concepts for Living and Dying
****
Volume 3
Unveiling the Hidden Instinct:
Understanding Our Interdimensional Survival Awareness
****
Volume 2: Keys to Self: Your Next Steps to YOU
****
Volume 1: Keys to Personal Discovery

BOOKLIST AND RECOMMENDED READING
Continued....

Ask Dr. Angela Series
Dr. Angela Brownemiller

—

The Bloodwin Code (Episode Books 1,2,3,4,5)
Dr. Angela Brownemiller

—

Seeing The Hidden Face Of Addiction
Dr. Angela Brownemiller

—

Gestalting Addiction
Dr. Angela Brownemiller

—

Contact us for information on the special
Science Fiction Series
on these consciousness and survival topics.
Email:

—

DrAngela@DrAngela.com

—

Note:
These books should be listed on Amazon.com and numerous other book distributor websites. If not finding these books on these sites and or in book stores, request these bookstores order these books, and or contact Amazon.com or Metaterra® Publications at Metaterra.com and/or DrAngela.com or the author, Dr. Angela Brownemiller. Check also under last name, Browne-Miller. Thank you.

ABOUT THE AUTHOR
Dr. Angela Brownemiller
Dr. Angela®

Dr. Angela Brownemiller, also known as Dr. Angela®, is an author, journalist, social thinker, clinician, psychotherapist, trainer, speaker, and creator of the ASK DR. ANGELA Series of broadcasts, podcasts, books, audiobooks, Ebooks, workshops, and programs. The views of Angela Brownemiller are centered on the great potential of the Human mind, heart, and soul, and on the rights of all of us, who and whatever we are (or think we are). Dr. Angela Brownemiller views the Human consciousness as a wealth of opportunity for exploration, insight, knowledge—and survival.

For more information on her work, see DrAngela.com and AskDrAngela.Help

The works of Angela Brownemiller are brought to you by:
METATERRA® PUBLICATIONS
(and numerous other publishers, see Amazon.com).

For copies of print books, audiobooks, and ebooks by this author,
see Amazon.com
or contact us at
DrAngela.com

To take part in our events and workshops,
and or
for personal consultations
in person or by telephone or online,
contact us at
DrAngela.com

VOLUMES 9 & 10 in the
KEYS TO CONSCIOUSNESS AND SURVIVAL SERIES
Written by Dr. Angela Brownemiller

Can we better understand the journeys we travel through in our lives? Can we detect and work with the patterns and processes we are forming, living within, and moving through? How much can we see about the patterns we form, and sometimes feel we cannot change, are caught in? How do we sensitize ourselves to the patterning processes we are engaged in? Find your way through the maze of life. See:

NAVIGATING LIFE'S STUFF:
DYNAMICS OF PERSONAL CHANGE, BOOK ONE
Seeing Our Processes and Their Patterns

NAVIGATING LIFE'S STUFF:
DYNAMICS OF PERSONAL CHANGE, BOOK TWO
Keys to Consciously Moving Through
Our Passages and Their Patterns

Now in Paperback, Audiobook, and Ebook forms.
Find these and other books by Dr. Angela Brownemiller
on Amazon.com and at DrAngela.com

Volume 4 in the
KEYS TO CONSCIOUSNESS AND SURVIVAL SERIES
HOW TO DIE AND SURVIVE
by Dr. Angela Brownemiller

YOUR RIGHT TO KNOW IS CLEAR. This far reaching, and life changing, book offers new ways of understanding ourselves and our lives. The author details progressive understandings and practices for moving into multi- and inter- dimensional consciousness and survival skills. Through use of metaphor, this author guides readers through: her progressive "shift" awarenesses; through LEAPs in understanding her sequential "shift technologies" by means of concepts, processes, and exercises contained in the chapters of this book. These exercises begin quite simply and carefully build toward some very esoteric understandings. ... This book overcomes limits to old models of what we are, who we are, and where we can be and go. Ultimately, this is an exploration of the infinite potential of our consciousness. Join us for the journey of your lifetime, or all your lifetimes.

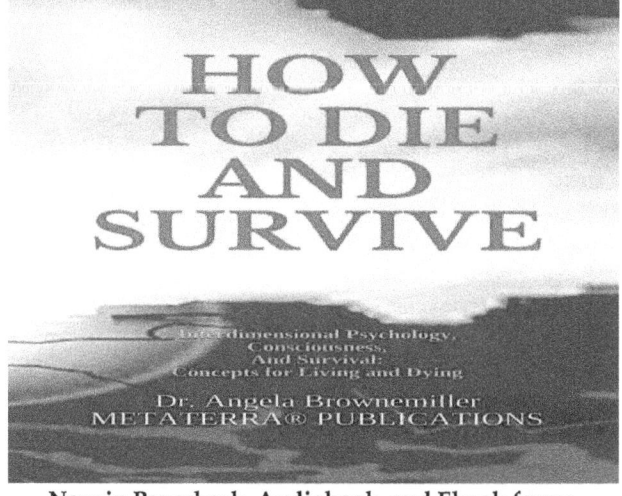

Now in Paperback, Audiobook, and Ebook forms.
Find these and other books by Dr. Angela Brownemiller
on Amazon.com and at DrAngela.com

Volume 3 in this
KEYS TO CONSCIOUSNESS AND SURVIVAL SERIES
UNVEILING THE HIDDEN INSTINCT
by Dr. Angela Brownemiller

Every day, we are presented with minor and major opportunities, reasons, even needs, to understand the nature of transitioning, shifting, from one state of mind, one way of being, one way of seeing the world, from one reality to another. In this sense, we are frequently calling upon ourselves to shift ourselves and our consciousness-es from one dimension of ourselves to another. At times, we may even sense that our well-being, perhaps even our survival, depends upon such a shift. ... Should we at some point find the survival level need to shift ourselves across ways of seeing the world, realities, dimensions, even perhaps from physical to non-physical and back, it is essential we have at least already considered the concepts involved. This book introduces, via metaphor, minor and major shift awareness-es, making these understandings accessible to us should we need these for everyday challenges as well as potentially profound survival reasons.

Now in Paperback, Audiobook, and Ebook forms.
Find these and other books by Dr. Angela Brownemiller
on Amazon.com and at DrAngela.com

Volume 10 in this
KEYS TO CONSCIOUSNESS AND SURVIVAL SERIES
SEEING BEYOND OUR LINE OF SIGHT
by Dr. Angela Brownemiller

SEEING BEYOND OUR LINE OF SIGHT: CONSCIOUSLY MOVING THROUGH LIFE'S CHANGES, TRANSITIONS, AND DEATHS ... is a simple yet profound book offering subtle yet major shifts in the way we think about changes, transitions, endings, and deaths. Here, we can see that we have the capability of holding and empowering our conscious selves as we move through events, changes, transitions, even emotional, even physical, death processes. ... The journey this book takes us on opens doors to finding our way through challenging, trying, even very difficult, events and passages in our lives. ... That we can survive is central as we undergo all minor and major transitions in our lives. ... Find yourself, know yourself, guide yourself through the minor and major transition and death processes you face during your life. You can define who and what you are for yourself. You can open this option in your mind, the option that you can develop this knowledge of yourself, and then carry this knowledge of yourself through this life, and perhaps also on beyond this lifetime. This is a key volume in the inspiring and fascinating KEYS TO CONSCIOUSNESS AND SURVIVAL SERIES.

SEEING BEYOND
OUR LINE OF SIGHT
Consciously Moving Through
Life's Changes, Transitions, And Deaths

Angela Brownemiller
METATERRA® PUBLICATIONS

Now in Paperback, Audiobook, and Ebook forms.
Find these and other books by Dr. Angela Brownemiller
on Amazon.com and at DrAngela.com

AUTHOR CONTACT:

DrAngela.com
DrAngelaBrownemiller@gmail.com

For
Paperback, Audiobook, and Ebook
versions of this and other books
by this author
Angela Brownemiller
see
Amazon.com

www.ingramcontent.com/pod-product-compliance
Lightning Source LLC
Chambersburg PA
CBHW051144030726

47504CB00004B/1037